G. J. FODE

ANOTHER NIGHT IN PARADISE

HARRY FOX IN THAILAND

In memory of Nang

Print: BOD GmbH, Norderstedt, Germany
ISBN 9783735742438

Contents

On the Prowl
They do have Wings
Money speaks louder than Words
The Clean Side of Dukdah
Fly me to the Moon
Little Miss Sao
Another Night in Paradise
Ah, and the Curvaceousness of Rainbow
Navy Day
The Golden Hour of Laan Sukapok

Low Season Blues
Country and Eastern
The Joy of Suffering (Vegetarian Delights)

Watching the Water fall
At Turning Point
Cutting the Cards

ANOTHER NIGHT IN PARADISE

A remark on "Another Night in Paradise"

Harry has trusted me with his Thai blogs and diaries for publication as I see fit, following the Nang accident he did not feel like going through the efforts of arranging editing and publishing the stuff himself.

Harry is a great narrator and I love his style, so I think it would be a crying shame not to let his readers in on his fabulous and sometimes ambidextrous life in "paradise". Surely Harry isn't always politically correct, but he gives you truth and candour flavoured with bold humour. For me personally his profound reasoning and pensive comments on life add a depth to the narrations that makes this book stand out among the numerous shallower recounts of the genre.

I am sure you will enjoy Harry's stories. For those of you who haven't heard of Harry before or would like to know a little more about him, I have added a short FAQ at the end of the book.

G. J. Fode, Phuket 2014

ANOTHER NIGHT IN PARADISE

1. IN THE PRESENCE OF BEAUTY

On the prowl
Awed in the presence of beauty, I offered her a drink

As I stepped out of the tuktuk (three-wheeled taxi) on Baramee Road only few metres from the Sandy Beach of Pakarang I noticed that the name on the sign was written in Thai only. So in this new but already funky place not many farangs could be anticipated. Farangs don't read Thai. So probably this was locals only.

สนุก

Paraphrased to English the name would be something like *Have a good time*. Now if that doesn't sound like the perfect beginning of a good night out!

"Halloh, come inside!"

I barely perceived the handsome man smiling at me, but I couldn't help notice the flashing teeth and the golden skin of the girl. Proceeding inside, she led me to a table and asked me what I would like to imbibe. In Thai, that is.

What a relief that the Thai words for *whisky* and *beer* are *wiskee* and *bia*. It makes cross-cultural communication so much easier. I ordered my favourite - Jack Daniel's. A bourbon? Jack Daniel's is not a genuine whisky, they say, because the Europeans own the term. But you won't ever see the word Bourbon on a bottle of Jack's. Tennessee whisky is the proper name and just like the Tennessee Waltz I guess it is supposed to strengthen brand reputation. Bourbon on the other hand is a French name, taken from the Bourbon family in New Orleans. While such arguments play an important role in the US and Europe, in Thailand they are wiped out by the omnipresent law of mai pen rai (who cares). Therefore, when ordering whisky in a Thai imbibery you better specify. If not, you never know what they are going to put on the table - it could be any liquid with a brownish colour, ranging from cheap, home brewed lao khao (rice booze) to a sublime Glenfiddich (and a bill to prove it).

Equally, maybe you would think that a Coffee Shop is a place like Starbucks to savour a good strong hot cup of coffee while you and your partner discuss the latest political and cultural topics. Well, nothing could be further from the truth. A real Thai style Coffee Shop serves everything but coffee (hence the name). Thai "whisky" is the game, Singha beer, spicy food and snacks. And then there is the action...

Imagine fair maidens clad in sparkling costumes that revealed their shapely figures... and for some reason the epic dresses all emphasise the butts. Long legs and high-heeled boots as important as the cordless microphone. Yes, microphone. They do sing, even if appearances come first...

As Coffee Shops go, the สนุก was rather humble. But the beauty of the performers on the little stage made me forget the bare walls and the plastic chairs right away. One charming songstress after the other climbed the platform to perform a short routine. You didn't have to understand Thai to know that this was all about the joy and preferable the pain of love.

Some people say that the singing abilities of the coffee shop girls resemble the artistic performances of a frog barking up a tree. I think that puts it rather rude. And anyway - who cares about technicalities, when the sheer sight of the entertainers makes your knees quiver! They have this enchanting mix of country girl naiveté paired with the sassiness of an alley cat. No siren could possibly be more alluring!

At the table next to mine a slender lady had seated herself. Meditatingly she took small sips from her glass of coke. She noticed my appraising glance and smile. I suddenly realized that I too needed a drink and gulped down two fingers worth of Tennessee whisky.

There must be a God in heaven, I thought. How can such beauty not be the brainchild of our Superior Creator! Gracefully, the girl rose from her chair, tucked at her mini-skirt and came over to my table. Did I feel all right? Why would I sit here so alone? Was it OK for her to sit down?

The girl's name was Dao, which means "star". And a star she was. Born 18 years ago in distant Isaan. Awed in the presence of so much beauty, I offered her a drink. Dao softly said that she only drank coke or plain water. Obviously she must be new and hadn't yet got into the knack of things.

"Sorry, I have to go" she said a few minutes later.

Strode onto the scene and brought a microphone up to her long-legged lips. Time ground to a halt. Dreams of tropical paradise with bamboo huts and coconut palms on pearly islands in emerald waters emerged in my mind as Dao slowly moved her hips to the rhythm of an Isaan song about love and pain.

Don't ask me what my dreams had to do with a singer in a Coffee shop. I don't know. Like all the other performers, Dao only sang one song at a time. Then she stepped down and headed right back for my table. She thanked me for the flowers and bowed her head in an elegant wai. "You are so beautiful" I heard myself say. "Kap khun kah" (thank you) Dao whispered demurely and actually even blushed a little. I suddenly understood that Divine Power had intervened and I was on my way to spend the rest of my life eternally in love with starry Dao.

Well, I didn't really want this to happen. I knew that I had only approximately sixty seconds to get out of blossomly Dao's siren powers before giving in to temptation and forever stay under her spell. So I hurriedly paid my bills, gave her a tip and got ready to go. It was not easy to leave charming Dao, who waved me good-bye with a ravishing smile.

"Please come again" were her last words.

I felt certain that I would. I felt like marrying her and have a dozen babies in a bamboo hut with falling coconuts on the beach of a pearly coral island. Still foolish after all those years in Thailand...

It was a hot night. I mopped the sweat from my forehead. Suddenly I remembered how it was to be a tourist in this place. Small wonder that thousands of farangs wanted to capture their enchanted hours in amazing Thailand for ever - at any price...

Her name was Noi and she slipped into my arms like a cat on a pillow.

After all those rhinestone girls at the karaoke where you *Have a good time* I felt like a dose of real Go Go action to blow some stardust off my brains. With Dao's slowly swaying hips and her short red dress in the back of my mind, I walked around the corner. It was around eleven. The beach road was brimming with strolling, shopping and laughing people. Filipino bossa from the Wallpaper and sacred music from the temple dance band at Thara Sala mingled with the sharp smell of burned chili and the soft fragrance of incense. The moon hung in the sky like the heavy bowl of a golden scale. Hey - it felt good to be alive in this place!

I passed the Irish Bar - fond memories of little Sansuk and her warm lips, who introduced me to the pleasures of Pakarang years ago. She was a devoted smoker then… I briefly wondered where she was now? Surely not in the Irish. Most girls passed through, because they got bored, or left, because they found a farang to pay for the rest of their lives.

I passed through the hollers of the girls (helloh, where you goh?), turned left at the Kings Fashion and patted the Grillhuette girl on her shapely bottom. You know the one that always stands on the corner with a menu and a smile? I know she is a respectable girl and you're not supposed to do that. Pat her. But I never could resist this one. She just looks so great with her tight dress, tight butt and tight everything.

"Next year I'm going to marry you" I whispered in her ear.

Her answer was a laugh and a smack in my belly. What had I expected? The phrase "next year" was a standing joke, of course. They all say that when leaving, and no matter how many tears they shed - you will never see them again. But thus are the morals of Pakarang. Nobody scolds you for patting a girl's - any girl's - bottom. Especially not when you are a farang. Like most Thais, Pakarang people are forgiving. Even more so. A pat on the bottom is always a compliment. And don't think I am talking jive.

At one of my visits to the mayor's office the deputy pulled up the gown of his secretary to show me her great legs and patted her bottom. And she wasn't even his mia noi (second wife). Goes to show you how much we appreciate sanuk (fun) in this country.

Dropping into the Cat Club with its soothing air-con, it felt like coming home. I tucked into my favourite corner, ordered a beer and enjoyed. Wasn't this a sore for sight eyes!

Buttocks and bikinis, what a feast! Right away one of the buttocks and bikini girls seated herself beside me. Did I mind? Hell - would you?

Her name was Noi and she slipped into my arms like a cat on a pillow. I had to by her a drink of course. Mangos may be cheap, but nothing is free. That is the second all overruling law in Thailand - farang always pays. Actually it shouldn't come as a surprise. *There ain't no such thing as a free lunch.* Why in the world would anybody expect this not to apply in a world where sex is the name and money the game?

But fact is, a lot of farangs will find out late. They never expect bar girls to be canny advertisers, but they are foolishly wrong. These girls are experts in presale sampling demonstrations. Even up to a point where the buyer is left without the money and without the prize.

As for me - being expat I was far beyond such considerations. Cosily cuddled up with shapely Noi, I watched the fire show. What a way to set your cigarette on fire! I have never figured out how they do this without getting burned and blistered in exquisite places.

"Can you do that?" I asked Noi.

She shuddered. "No! Too hot!"

She leaned back. I felt her hand on my thigh. At the next table Wolfgang and Erich waved at me. I knew them well. They had been visiting Pakarang off and on as long as I could remember.

"Halloh mister Fox" Erich yelled in his heavy German accent "How is ze businez?"

I pointed at Noi and Erich let out a howling laugh. What was there to say? Were we having fun already?

Basically I could have stayed in the Club all night, get drunk and let them carry me into a tuktuk at closing hour. But I hadn't been out for a while - several days in fact - and I felt like exploring a bit.

So I bid buxom Noi farewell with a peck on her cheeks and got out. A man's got to do what he's got to do. Farewell Noi, please don't cry! I'm sure there are many farangs waiting to cuddle with you.

I felt like cruising on up to Bangla Road via Soi Crocodile and check out what was happening there.

The irony of the tall "ladies" with their unbelievable curves versus small male bartenders never escaped me.

I cut through the back lawn to Soi Crocodile, arriving at the lavatory. I just love this narrow archway that leads to the bar-alley. Two people have to turn sidewise in order to pass. Which is nice, if the one person is me and the other a shapely Thai girl.

Anyway, the Crocodile Disco is gone now and what's left are any amount of equally bellicose kathoeys just waiting for a lonely Fox to come along so they can embrace his manhood with eager lips and sink their shiny teeth into his wallet.

Interspersed between the kathoey A Go Go on one end and the Tequila Bar on the other were a dozen bars with "real" girls. The sport being, of course, that a non-specialist would have a hard time figuring out whether he was talking to a lady, a boy, or a *ladyboy*. Most of the bars feature huge wooden chopping blocks and a hammer. I spotted a group of Korean tourists trying to hit heads with the sharp end of the hammer. I admit it helps when you are drunk.

Not that you hit the nails better. But it is more fun, because the hammer slips and crashes the Singha beer bottles.

I bulldozed through the crowd at the Tequila Bar (adequately named so because you get served everything but Tequila - I guess you are getting the pattern) pushed an old, legless man from his barstool and joined the spectators for a while.

I say, this little platform in the middle of TB must be the best entertainment value for your money in Pakarang (there is no fee, of course). Incredible, what has happened on that tiny stamp of a "stage" in my days. I have seen three stark naked "girls" arranging amazing body parts and limbs in wondrous ways.

The irony of the tall "ladies" with their unbelievable curves up on the platform versus the small, skinny, all male bartenders never escaped me. If it were my bar, I would rename it "Small Bartenders and Big Kathoeys Bar". Which is a bad name for a bar, really, which goes to show that I'm probably better off to stick with the drinking and writing business, not the bar business.

As all the bass speakers except one were busted, the music in the Tequila was so loud and tinny it made your ears ring the rest of your holiday.

Which is good, because now you could turn a deaf ear on every kathoey that wants you to take her photo and shove a hundred Baht note down her circular silicones.

As the alcohol went in, my desires grew. Already not only the katheoys started looking good, but every piece

of buttock in tight shorts that drifted by under my nose.
So I figured it was time to retreat to a secure place...

They do have Wings

Uan made it clear that she had never kissed a farang before. As I had never met a Go Go dancer who had never kissed a farang before I decided to take her out.

I don't really know why they called it "Rock Hard". Except for one thing. Ah - so we are talking fornication again! Not Thai people that is, they pronounce it "lock heart", which definitely has a different ring to it. Can't seem to make up my mind whether the Hard Rock Downstairs A Go Go or the Cowboy A Go Go Upstairs has the better ambience for fornication. Basically the classical outfit of the Rock Hard dancers are the sexier of the two. Nothing in this world beats Thai ladies in French underwear, I swear.

But a big plus goes to the Cowboy Go Go for trying to do something different. So that's where I get my daily exercise, right there, running up and down the stairs between Rock and Cowboy girls. In the meantime my old friend Stephen sits outside in the BBQ, talking to the police guys, who have chosen Rock Hard their second home. Stephen hardly goes into the Go Go's any more, except when he has to take a leak.

"I go to Bangkok so often" he says "it is much better there!"

But he is wrong, of course. Nothing is better in Bangkok. Everything is better in Pakarang. An evening out in Bangkok begins and ends with sitting in a taxi, looking at traffic. In between you sit in another taxi, driving from one place to another, looking at more traffic. There is nothing at all which can compare to the uniqueness of Pakarang. Here you wander around in one long, happy intoxication from one bar, one A Go Go to another until your good old Asian mule, the Honda Dream, takes you home somehow, somewhere. Sometimes you wake up at your own house, sometimes alone. Sometimes you wake up at somebody else's. Or in a hotel. But there is always your good old Honda Dream parked outside, waiting.

This particular night my favourite dancer, Bui, was not among the Cowboy rompers. Maybe she was with a farang. Maybe she had found another job. You never know. One day they are here, the next day they are gone. But there was another girl, who caught my eye. Right away she made a point out of dancing "just for me"... you know, how they can do that? Look at you, smile and never take their eyes away until you actually feel like blushing and buy them a drink?

This new girl's name was Uan (thick). Which stroke me as kind of strange, because she was very lean and neat. But in a country where parents even name their kids Moo (pig) I guess Uan is not too bad. When Uan stepped down to shake hands with me, the rim of her Stetson was exactly the level of my forehead. I was seated and she was standing up. Involuntarily I wondered if one could not put the hat to some good use, like placing a drink on it? Then Uan kissed me and I understood that cowboy hats are good for donating shelter while kissing a Go Go dancer on the lips in her bar.

Uan made it clear that she had never kissed a farang before. As I had never met a Go Go dancer who had never kissed a farang before I decided to take her out. I tried to haggle about the bar fine. As a regular customer I felt entitled to a discount.

But it was a no go.

"We ought to charge you extra" the tab keeper said, shaking her head. "We will soon have to replace the worn out steps of the stairs! Are you going to pay for that?" she added, trying to look morose. We had discussed my wandering habit.

So I took my newly found beloved one downstairs, treading very carefully on the steps. Stephen was still sitting with the MIB (men in black).

As he saw us, he exclaimed: "Harry, where did you find that one?"

"In the Cowboy A Go Go" I said "Maybe Pakarang is not so bad after all?"

Stephen looked at us with a mischievous grin. "I can't believe I didn't see her first."

Uan took his hand and smiled. "Mai pen rai, I will see you later."

Her smile was like an open flower. You could tell that she very much wanted Stephen to be the second farang in her life, whom she had ever kissed.

I decided to split and tucked Uan away from the old hoodlum. Leaving the Rock Hard, we headed for Soi Sunset.

When you slip into Extasy, you know you made the right choice. That's the motto on their logo.

I sure felt I had made the right choice when I slipped into Extasy with Uan's little hand in mine! She looked different now. The Stetson was gone, she had put on a long black dress and let the hair fall down her back. She sat there like a mahogany statue with one hand under her chin, looking at the dancers with great apprehension. I ordered a coke for her and - you guessed it - a Jack Daniel's for my old self. Leaning back in the arms of love I let my eyes roam. It was cool in here. I wondered absentmindedly how the girls kept their warmth. I mean, they were not moving that much. The name of the place might be Extasy, but the dancing style between the shining poles on the floor was still the classical - and slow - Thai A Go Go. Which means their belly part of the body moving forward and backward with this wavy, bumpy motion that rocks the whole body except the head and the feet. A classical Thai Go Go dancer will nod her head gently, grab the pole with two outstretched hands and twist her feet sidewise.

The foot twist is especially fascinating. I doubt you will see it anywhere else. I used to stand like that when I was a teenage boy because I had seen James Dean do it and it ruined my shoes. To see the Extasy dancers do it was something quite different of course. The first thing is - the heels were so high, you can't believe it can be done without breaking either them or the ankles. At the same time they go down a little bit and spread their knees, which makes the whole posture look wildly erotic. It is a mixture between awkward devotion and ultimate control. Far out.

I could tell by the look on sweet Uan's face she figured she had something to learn. I patted her shoulder and told her that nobody looked as good as her own sweet self up on second floor with a cowboy hat and a tight pair of torn shorts.

"Thank you" she said and gave me a little wai "I know you are being polite!"

"No I am not" I said "I am not just being polite. When I saw you up there, I saw an angel."

"What is an angel?" she asked.

"An angel is..." I hesitated, pondering how to explain the unexplainable. I mean, how do you explain what an angel is to somebody called Uan from Isaan, who knows about Phees (Thai ghosts) only and who has just kissed her first farang...?

"They are like airplanes" I said "Or more like butterflies."

Uan shook a finger under my nose. "I am not a butter-fly!"

Being a Thai person, to her the word butterfly had negative connotations. Can you believe that? Thais must be the only people in the whole world that associate butterflies with ugly cheaters.

"Like a female Buddha with wings."

By the look she gave me I saw that I had convinced Uan I was dingdong (crazy). I gave it a last try.

"Like creatures from heaven" I said "You know, from up above...?"

"What is heaven?" Uan asked.

Number 6 was doing her thing. A couple of black'n heavy Navy boys hollered and couldn't believe what they saw.

Extasy made a point out of having a cool air con and a powerful but deep PA system, not the usual screeching tweeters. Which suited me fine because Uan and I were actually able to speak to each other through the bump and grind of the loudspeakers. This is a thing I noticed about the Extasy since my first visit about a zillion years ago. They crank up the bass, but not the drilling squeech of the treble units. Which makes the music a physical sensation instead of a pain in the ear. Maybe they should change their motto to: *When you slip into Extasy you know your ears will survive!*

"You are an angel" I repeated myself for another try.

"The bible says angels are messengers. That's why they have these wonderful wings, you know. The fly back and forth, bringing messages from God to his people."

Uan looked at me in awe.

"They really have wings...?" she whispered.

"Yes, they really have wings. And they shelter you with those great wings in order to let no harm come to you."

"Do Thai people have angels too?"

"No" I said "Thais don't *have*, they *are*. Thai girls are angels. You are an angel. That is why farangs come here and spend their money on you - to be kissed by an angel."

"But I no have wings!" Uan exclaimed.

"Yes, you do! You just can't see them. Only farang humans can see the wings of an angel."

Uan laughed and revealed two perfect rows of shiny teeth.

"You joking me!"

She gave me a slap on the back.

"You joking me! There are no such things."

She was wrong, you know. There are angels. And Uan was one - to me she was, at least.

I didn't really want to sit in Extasy talking about angels all night. I had dirtier things in mind. Angel or no angel, I had seen Uan rock her raccoons up there at the Cowboy place. So I grabbed her little hand and dragged her down bustling Soi Bangla. Down Soi Eric - passing all those *helloh, where you goh*s!

On the way to Flash a Go Go you'll have to battle the Scylla and Charybdis of Pakarang. Two hundred lovely ladies to each side, yelling, reaching, grabbing. Besides a few dreamers just sitting there, building castles out of dreams - wooden blocks that is. To tell you the truth, running the gauntlet through Soi Eric up to Flash A Go Go is one of the good parts. No man can say it doesn't do anything for his manhood walking down an alley full of beautiful ladies crying out for him and not be lying. Normally it is kind of difficult to find excuses for not sitting down with a gorgeous girl that woos you that much. But Soi Eric is different. You can point straight ahead and say "Flash A Go Go" and they'll understand.

Another good part is the staircase leading up to the Flash. Two people can hardly pass. It is narrow; it is steep and looks like something out of an old Brooklyn alley.

"Jacob's ladder."

"What?" said Uan.

"Stairway to heaven, sweetie. Home of the angels."

At the door this quaint sign *No outside beers*. I took my outside beer inside once. But that wasn't what it meant.

A lovely lady in underpants opened the door. We were gazing directly into her slip, her welcoming smile hovered way over our head, because we were still standing on a lower step on them steep stairs.

Once inside I occupied my favourite chair at the back, right next to the ladies "dressing room". Which is not a dressing room, but only the small corner next to the loudspeakers.

Uan the angel sat down by my side and struck her characteristic pose: hand under chin, eyes wide open, gawking at the girls.

Now we were talking! A Fox felt like a fish in water - or rather in a burrow. Slip into Flash and you know you're in for a good time. I ordered Jack Daniel's and a beer to chase it with.

Number 69 was doing her thing.

A couple of black'n heavy Navy boys hollered and they couldn't believe what they saw.

"Man" I heard one of them say "if she can do that with a pen, what couldn't she do with my (beep)!"

Time flies fast when you sit and drink Jack Daniel's and beer in Flash A Go Go. I had been so absorbed, first by Number 69 and her pen, then by Number 112 and her incredibly small tanga and since by my old friend Lek, who cried my name out loud when she saw me.

She had come back to town the week before from a long stay in Nakhon Nowhere with her mother, her sisters, brothers, uncles, aunts, their wives and husbands and water buffaloes.

Time flew on. Later, when I found Lek sitting on my lap I noticed that Uan the angel had disappeared. But I didn't worry. That is just the thing about angels, you see, they come and go according to their own laws and logistics. Maybe she had gotten a call from somebody who needed a lean angel with two perfect rows of shining teeth even more urgently than me.

I just hoped it wasn't Stephen.

Money speaks louder than words!

I didn't recognise her at first. She looked different without the fancy clothes and the make-up.

At five in the morning Lek wasn't looking that sharp. Her eyes were closed and if the music hadn't been so loud I could've heard her snoring. But then again, she had gone through rough times. It was low season, there were only few farangs around and she had not yet operated in this particular field long enough to work up any number of boyfriends to send her a solid stream of money from abroad.

In spite of her girlish looks Lek was a mature woman, you see. She had three kids to take care of and an old father, who was working up horrendous hospital bills way back in Chiang Rai. Her husband had disappeared with somebody else one day and left the complete menagerie to Lek. I knew Lek had been on the chase several days in a row, never slowing down. It was understandable that she was tired.

All around us the sights and sounds of late-night Pakarang were flashing and wailing. I ordered another Jack Daniel's, fought off a couple of farang-starved girls and leaned back. I sat and kind of meditated while everybody were doing their thing. Slowly the level of whisky in the bottle sank close to the bottom. It felt good in a strange way to just sit there and watch Lek curled up in her bamboo chair like a kitten. Every once in a while a bartender would bring me some ice.

Then, abruptly, the power went and Pakarang was transformed into a black well of darkness. A hundred mouths cried out at the same time. Lighters were enkindled, candles put on fire and one of the bars had a temporary flashlight on. Lek awoke and let her eyes roam like a hare's.

"Harree..." she exclaimed "what you do?"

"No no" I said "it's not me, we have a fei dab (power failure)".

"Ah..." she sighed.

In the flickering light of a candle she looked so young. Almost like a frightened child.

"It is all right" I heard myself saying "I'm going to take you home!"

She began to gather her things - purse, keys, hair brush - right away.

"Where you motobike?"

I ordered the bill and thought things over. I wasn't really prepared to spend the rest of the night - or rather the following morning - with Lek. I just felt I ought to bring her home and let her get some sleep. But when I sensed her slim body leaning onto my not so slim body and her bare arms around my not so slim waste, vows disappeared.

We rode up Sai Nam Yen, passed Vises Hotel and Andy's Umbrella Hut, which was still open. Lek's bungalow sat in a row of new buildings in a soi (street) off Nam Yen. Everything was still new and shiny. As we passed the last corner, I heard someone call out my name. I looked back and it was Dao.

Yes, Dao, the starry-lipped singer from the Coffee-shop with the name that meant something like *Have a good time*. I almost did not recognize her at first - she looked different without the shining clothes, the make-up and the boots. Dao beckoned me to come, obviously she had something to show me.

I hesitated. What about Lek? But then Lek said: "No ploblehm. I go sleep, you come later!"

She hopped off the bike and disappeared into her bungalow. I followed Dao into her room. She smiled and revealed these white teeth that took me back to the coffee shop, where she used to stand with long legs and all.

"So how is work?" I asked.

"Fine!" she said "Very fine! Everything is good."

She made it sound like it was not good at all.

"I will show you something!"

Dao grabbed my hand and dragged me off to the bedroom. There she sat down on the bed without letting go of my hand. I looked around. A bed, a close-hanger, a picture of the King on the wall.

"What do you want to show me?" I asked.

Dao shook her head a little and pulled me closer. Her eyes were black pearls in a nightly forest, beyond her lips lay the promise of eternal bliss. I felt her sweet breath on my nose. Longingly my lips touched hers. Bluntly Dao jerked her face back.

"What's the matter?" I asked.

"No no, sorry!" Dao exclaimed.

She flung both her arms around my neck and covered my cheek with kisses.

"I sorry! I want you, okay?"

Feverishly she began to take off her clothes, exposing a black bra.

Even through the haze of my drunkenness I sensed that this was not right. I turned to go.

"I'll come back tomorrow, okay?"

Dao leaped towards the door and blocked my way. "Please" she begged "don't go! Stay with me tonight, okay? Don't you like me? I have big tits, you see! Since I had baby they are very big!"

She opened her bra. I drew a deep breath.

"I like you Dao. Even more than that, I think you are very sweet and very beautiful, but..."

"Okay, then stay!"

Her lips were in my face again, her tender body scented of temple flowers. Like two kitten in the Garden of Eden we floated in space. The airy sound of the fan transmuted into heavenly strings. How could somebody I knew so little about know so much about my deepest desires? I stroke her peachy cheeks.

And got wet fingers. Dao was crying. I wanted to look at her face, but she tried to hide it with her hands.

"Listen sweetheart" I said "this does it! What is the matter? C'mon, you can tell me!"

"Please, don't ask" she sobbed "Mai pen rai, it is not important!"

She tried to hold me once again, but it was too late. She couldn't stop the tears and the sorrow. Her face - once so sweet and happy, had turned into a mask of Asian agony.

Finally, through sobs and moans, out came the story. Dao's mother back in Isaan had been on a bus one not so lucky day. Trying to avoid a head on collision with a truck, the driver made a sudden turn and the bus landed way down in a ditch. Two people died, the driver fled the scene and now her mother had a broken back and no money to get it fixed.

So Dao decided to do what everybody had told her was the only solution. But it wasn't easy. She was disgusted by men who were much older than her and she didn't have the psyche to go through the rituals of the game.

She tried to get drunk, but the alcohol only made her vomit and gave her a headache. She got fired from the coffee shop because she failed to show up...

So. Finally Harry Fox James came along. And even though I had been riding with Lek on the pillion, Dao had decided to try he luck with her special one - which was me!

I looked down on her sad face with those sweet red lips and black eyes. There was only one thing to do...

Yas, she said, and I make luhve like a labbit, too.

If I ever met a hardcore coffee-shop worshipper, Wolfgang from Switzerland was it. Whenever he was on Phuket, he would spend hours and hours of night-time exploring the countless number of coffee shops on the island. Later he would ramble on for even more hours about the beauty and the natural charm and the what-yagotnot of these wonderfully amazing girls. But he was also a gentleman. And he was good looking. But most of all - he was rich.

So the next day I introduced Dao to Wolfgang. It was like a setting out of a Hollywood Romance movie. In the soft light of wrought iron lamps the well-kept lawn glowed like a green carpet. In the roofed outdoor section Wolfgang was waiting for us already. There was a huge bunch of flowers on the table. Red roses for a blue lady.

When Dao and I entered the garden, Wolfgang jumped out of his chair like a jack-in-a-box. Starry-eyed Dao approached him like a diva in slow-motion. A mild breeze made her dark hair fly in flows like waves in the Andaman Sea. And you know - unhurriedly Dao walked right up to Wolfgang, dropped her eyes, bent her knees and gave him an impeccable wai. As I said - pure Hollywood stuff. It took no more than ten minutes before the two love birds were so totally engaged in each other that I figured I'd might as well leave. And I did. I don't think they even noticed.

The next thing was to figure out what to do about Lek. What she really wanted was a husband. Not just any husband, but someone who would take care of her children as well. For a second I opted to make her Wolfgang's mia noi (second wife). But just for a second. It would never work out. Or maybe it would - but not right now, while he was busy romancing a blue lady with red roses and Andaman Sea waves for hair. I would have to ponder the matter.

There is no better place to ponder whether you should make a girl named Lek somebody's mia noi or give her a two-year's scholarship for Christmas than the Congo Bar. The sun was sinking low. Its golden rays wrapped Soi Bangla in a flaxen blanket. The street was still comparatively quiet. I sat down at one of the tables close to the pool-desk and watched the girls play. It was too early for straight whisky, so I ordered coke and manau (lime) with my Jack Daniel's. One of the girls shot some good balls, I noticed. And speaking of balls - her physical appearance wasn't too bad, either. When she bowed down over the green cloth and stood still for concentration, she was the very picture of vigilant beauty. All in all it was a pleasure to see her do her thing and when she asked me to join the game I gladly took the opportunity to show off my balls a little bit and to get acquainted.

As it happened, the girl's name was Tay.

"Thai?"

"No, Tay as in Katay."

"Oh! Rabbit. I see."

"Yas" she said "and I make luhve like a labbit, too."

She stroke up a hearty laughter. "But I play pool like a senake (snake)."

I cannot say whether fair Tay made love like a rabbit. But she certainly did not play pool like a snake. As I said, she shot some pretty straight balls.

As I watched the spheres dance, a girl named Lek stayed in the back of my mind. Why could you not play the game of life like a game of pool? Every angle has its opportunities, every number has to go.

Tay was looking down her cue with concentration shining out of her eyes.

Zonk! She set the white ball spinning perfectly, number six went down with a smack. Then I heard somebody call my name.

It was Reinhard, the owner of the bar. He grabbed my hand and shook it like the bodybuilder he is. That the German do a lot. Shake hands, I mean.

A couple of years ago the Congo Bar had the literally strongest line-up of Pakarang bargirls ever. All the Congos seemed to be plump, muscular or heavy set girls with a squeezer of a handshake at that time. Maybe Reinhard the bodybuilder had picked them to his taste. Walking by on the narrow boardwalk presented a real danger then. If you refused to come in and the girls really wanted you to, they would just grab and drag you and bind you to the stake in the middle of the room.

Reinhard laughed.

"Yes" he said "actually we did have some strong women back then, didn't we. And didn't you actually date one of them, what was her name, Toy...Koy...?"

He looked at me quizzically.

I changed the subject. No need to go into details of old bygone times.

"I know this girl..." I began.

"...and you love her too much" Wolfgang chimed in.

"No no, it's like this..."

I told Wolfgang Lek's story. Wolfgang listened and said, finally: "Sure, bring her in. I have a place where she can stay, I'll even give her a basic salary. We'll fix her up in no time. Pretty soon she will meet a rich guy from overseas and all her troubles will be forgotten."

Tay the "labbit" was patiently waiting for our conversation to finish. I took my cue. This was it - time to hit the eightball.

Smack! Neatly and nicely the ball landed in the designated corner. Tay grinned. She had lost, she would have to pay for the beer. I kind of suggested that we could make an arrangement, where money did not come into play as such... But she refused laughingly.

"Samall manee (small money)" she said, and I had to agree. As they say: Nern poot gwah kham - money speaks louder than words. But - it has to be a reasonable amount. For a moment I considered whether I actually should do some talking to little Rabbit with a reasonable amount of nern (money). But I decided against it. Not right now. The evening was young, the bottle of whisky still full, and the pool-table was waiting for another round.

A couple of days later in Soi Seadragon I met Lek again.

She dug me in the ribs and said: "You didn't come back to me that night. So now you love Dao, eh?"

"Not really" I said "It's just that Dao had this problem and she asked me to help..." Lek laughed.

"So you gave her some "help" and she forgotten the problem, eh?"

I wondered whether it was possible for me to get across that I did not have any private relationship with Dao. On the other hand, it didn't seem important, either.

"So what about you?" I asked. I told her about the job in the Congo bar. Lek listened attentively. I was repeating Wolfgang's last words about meeting a rich farang, when Lek turned her head. Somebody was just coming into the bar.

"Oh" she cried out "Harree, meet my new boyfriend!"

It was Wolfgang, the coffee-shop worshipper from Switzerland.

I must have looked rather silly. Wolfgang laughed and said: "Close your mouth Harry! Your gold-teeth are showing!"

"But, aren't you supposed to be with Dao?" I gasped.

"Ah, yes Dao."

Wolfgang shook his head.

"You know what is funny. We had a wonderful night. The moon, the food, the champagne... Then Dao insisted in taking me to her apartment and I basically thought that we were - how do you say this in English *ein Herz und eine Seele?*"

"On the way to get married" I said.

"Yes, like that, on the way to get married. But when I tried to kiss her, she shied back and said that she had somebody in her life already. I went out to smoke a cigar on the banner balustrade of her balcony and suddenly I saw her!"

He pointed at Lek, who beamed back like a Christmas tree.

"And the rest is going to be a history, as they say."

"And the rest is history" I corrected automatically.

I was baffled, not sure I understood.

So what had happened to Dao, I wondered, and why had she refused to patch up with Wolfgang?

I was kind of busy for the next few days. But as soon as I had the time I went to see Dao in the little soi off Sai Nam Yen. The house was still there, but Dao was gone. I asked the girls next door and they said she had left for Bangkok.

Bangkok...?

"Yes, her husband came and took her with him."

Her husband...?

The girls looked at me as the stupid farang I was. Yes, her husband! Didn't I know that Dao had a rich husband, who was in charge of Siam Commercials, one of the biggest trading companies of Thailand?

Right that instant I saw a somewhat familiar face peering out of a door further down the alley. It was Tay, the rabbit, who played pool like a snake.

"I didn't know you lived here, too."

"Yas" she replied "I see you, but you busy butterfly with Lek and Dao."

I wondered if I should try to explain to fair Rabbit that I had no personal involvement with neither Lek nor Dao but it didn't seem worth the effort. Looking at her beautiful smiling face - that bore no resemblance to a rabbit's at all - I decided instead that it would be much more worth an effort trying to see whether she really made *luhve like a labbit*.

The Clean Side of Dukdah

The next day I woke up in a different house.

Old Pakarang Hands just say "the trap". Don't ask me why ;-) The Banana was the first disco in Pakarang and it still drew a steady crowd that liked to hang out here and strut their stuff till the wee hours of the morning.

Referred to as "Banana Girls" the ladies there were much sought after by a young German and Italian clientele because they were fun loving, action minded and generally rather pretty by European standards. Some even quite young, around early twenty.

Maybe it comes as a surprise to you that "young" by Pakarang standards is around twenty. Some tourists believe they can find teenagers or even children in the streets of Pakarang. But that is not possible. The only children that rove around at night are the flower and chewing gum kids. Not that they are working here by choice, but they too are under strict supervision, believe me. As a visitor, you might not notice the old lady sitting on a log of cement, watching her little work force with apparent indifference, nor the young hoodlum in the corner with the inconspicuous shirt... But they are the mamasan and the police officer who watch and notice and know every little detail of what is going on. Don't be fooled by their looks, the police guy packs a thirty-eight and the mamasan drives a heavy knuckle. And these two are not the only ones. A whole squadron of mamasans and undercover police officers are at large here, there, everywhere and at all times. Tourists do not know that there are practically no mafia nor pimps in most parts of Thailand. Certainly in Pakarang you will find neither.

Why is that? you may ask.

Well the answer is simple: the police act as both police AND mafia. So whoever wants to erect an illegal or for some reason not quite sober business, will have to go directly to the police. No need to escrow - bribe the person who is in charge, the police officer himself. And so the police know all and will act relentless in order to keep rules, written or unwritten, and power lines intact.

Thus in regard to legal age and tourism the laws are strict and the enforcement fierce. Every girl carries her ID card. Firstly she may be scrutinised any time by an undercover police man (who is not undercover to her, if she has been around for some time) and secondly she will not be allowed to the hotels where tourists live. No hotels, no business.

So you won't find any girl under the legal age - which is 18. Thailand is very conscious of its image as tourist destination. What Thais do in their own native brothels and parlours is a different story altogether - but neither the tourists nor the press ever go there. For one thing, most brothels do not advertise at all, and if they do, you will see some inauspicious sign in Thai letters, so a stranger will never know where to find those secret spots that are obvious and well known to any Thai person, even if they are sitting right under his nose disguised as snack store, massage joint or barber shop...

Anyway, the Banana was a traditional disco and not a girly bar. So you don't have to pay a bar fine when you pick someone up. The name of the game is to pretend you just dropped into the disco for a dance and a beer. Accidentally you meet this young beautiful lady, mutual attraction arises and you decide to spend a dance and a drink together. Maybe even two dances and two drinks. Or maybe the whole night...

Now I am not an old square. But it is not always the pumped up volume and hazardous speed that makes my fun. My ears were still hurting after the Tequila Bar screech so after a quick drink I decided to split and head on down to Soi Sunset.

It was running kind of late, so everybody on the streets was gravitating towards Soi Sunset. I followed the stream of black-haired ladies in black dresses and golden shoes up Bangla Road to the Vienna Bar.

It was night, but hot, as always. Thirsty after the sweaty walk I climbed a barstool and with the last bit of will power I ordered a Jack Daniel's and a beer to go with it. I relaxed a little while my blood pressure returned to normal. Out of the corner of my eyes I noticed the soccer game on the monitor, when...

There she was! Do you remember Manfred Mann? *Doo wah diddy...*? Well, old Manfred didn't know it back then, but this was the girl he was singing about. Pink tank top and a sweatshirt tucked beneath the waist. Showing a lot of skin and a navel like a fingerprint in almond paste. She was just standing there (remember the Beatles? *I saw her standing there?)* lost in a world of her own, swaying softly to the music.

I took a swing at my whisky and enjoyed the sight. I surely am neither the first not the last person to be stricken by the remarkable beauty of Thai ladies. And through the years I assure you, brother, I have seen stunners in troops. But still my heart skips a beat and I feel a tiny twitch in my stomach when I see a Thai lady that in such a beautiful way allegorises the glory of God the Creator. She was shooting alone, but patrons and girls were streaming in from the downtown bars. As the joint geared up, two other girls stepped in to play. All around the table it was tits and almond paste navels, round butts and shapely legs. If this had been a lounge in New York, a disco in Miami or a nightclub in Paris you might be cautious or even overpowered and would have to consider your openings carefully. But this was Pakarang. Glory was everywhere and beauty nothing but routine. Living in a paradise with feather beds as floor plates you lose the fear of flying.

So I walked over to God's allegory and asked if I could join the play. She smiled invitingly, let me go on for a little while, scrutinising my style before letting loose and giving me a hard time.

But I won the game and she immediately took revenge. In between shooting balls she told me her story. Born and raised in the poor province of Isaan she had left her home at the tender age of 18 to seek fame and fortune in fair Phuket. She had been working as a waitress in a Thai restaurant, where she was paid only three thousand Baht a month. Her mother had fallen sick and her brother had had a motorbike accident in Chiang Mai, so now she was looking for a well-paid job because her poor family had only her to rely on. Her friends had suggested that she might try her luck as a bargirl. Today was the first time she ever had ventured into the noisy, happy nightlife of Pakarang. I felt genuine compassion for the little thing and offered her a beer, wondering where she had learned to shoot the ball that well.

"No no" she said "I drink Black Label only! Good for headache." So we fell into each other's arms and lovely Dukdah - that was her name - planted a lingering kiss on my lips. We shared a bottle of the brown stuff and by the time the bottle was empty I was kind of full. Lovely Dukdah looked me in the eye.

"You mau (drunk) already" she said.

I agreed. Maybe we better go home!

"You have my wife already?" she asked.

"No" I said "I have neither your wife nor my own!"

"Okay. Where is your hotel?"

At this point it became increasingly difficult for me to focus. I kind of hinted that I was a rich oil-sheik who stayed at the Royal Suite on Diamond Cliff. What happened later on is only a blur in my memory. I remember part of the tuktuk ride with lovely Dukdah and the wind in my drunken visage. But I don't recall the expression on her face or what she said when we arrived at my humble residence on Soi Nanai. I am sure the two of us had a good time. I vaguely remember her waking me up - and falling asleep again on the kitchen floor. Did I hear her asking me where the floor mop was?

I didn't have the strength to wonder about that. I mumbled something about stars and coffee shops and went right back to a perturbed sleep full of dreams about brown skinned sirens with almond paste bikinis.

The next day I woke up in a different house. Well, not really a different house. But a clean house. Truly clean. Effectively spick and span. Incredible. It hadn't looked like this since I moved in. I searched for Dukdah, but she wasn't there. She had left a lipstick note on my bathroom mirror, though.

It read: *Thank you to much, teerak. I go home see mother in hospital. Come back to you again.*

Now - there is a lot to be said about nightlife Pakarang. Sure. But whoever said it was dirty has never met my Dukdah.

Fly me to the Moon

For some reason Pakarang has these special nights

Once in a while a man has to blow sawdust from his brain. I personally find there is no better way to do that then to saddle a heavy chopper - preferably my Harley or Suzuki - and just let it run.

On this particular night I was riding my 1400 Intruder. Harleys are great, but the Intruders are something special. For one thing, they run smoothly as silk... their cylinders fire timely as a Swiss clockwork, whereas the Harleys with their one pin crankshaft fire the pistons irregularly. Another thing is the dependability of the Japanese ladies. I just didn't want to have an American breakdown in the middle of nowhere.

I had been out seeing the sights of the island most of the day wherever the bike would take me - and it occurred to me that a late evening ride around Pakarang would be a worthy final for a wonderful day. So I maneuvered the ponderous bike through Soi Seadragon trying not to hit anybody. I enjoyed the cheers and the hellohs of the girls and parked the chopper in the back at the Rasta Bar. You know, where the farang ladies hang out with the dreadlock guys.

My Polish friend Attila's old place is gone. No more Seadragon burgers. Attila is now doing what he always wanted to do: mend motorbikes. Instead it's a new A Go Go. I wondered if this one was going to be just as all the others, or if they'll dream up a new theme. The Classroom theme is taken as well as the Country. Maybe they should make it a Burger a Go Go? Supply the girls with plastic burgers around the waist and the bust.

Now the thing about Soi Seadragon is - not every bar stocks Jack Daniel's. But okay, I'm not a fanatic, don't believe what Stephen says about me. I wasn't going to stay for long, so I just grabbed an ice-cooled Carlsberg bia Chang at My Love Bar. But by chance boss Somchai himself graced the bar that night, so all of a sudden it was Johnny Walker and Cocktails and what do I know. No way he was going to let me go without spending a few drinks – and then some.

Somchai is one of these truly Thai-like persons in the sense of being helpful and sharing. He was the first Thai friend I ever made on Phuket. One of the first things he did, he took me to an oracle priest at Wat Chalong temple. I didn't understand anything at all and Somchai had to translate everything afterwards. And it was all wonderful stuff: I was going to make it big on Phuket, marry a wonderful girl and so on and so forth. Maybe Somchai made all of this up. But it didn't matter. His intentions were more than good.

"Have you come to my bar to look for female company?" he asked.

Somchai smiled and pointed at one of his girls.

"This one has just come in from Isaan" he said "She would make a very good wife for you!"

"Thank you Somchai" I said "but let it be. The last time I made somebody my wife, I ended up with alimony bills and a broken heart. It's going to be a while before I will get around to that again."

"No no" Somchai said gravely" you just have to find the right one!"

He waved one hand at one of the girls and shouted: "Eh, Jui! Come here, leoleo (quickly)! There's a farang here to see you!"

"Oh please, don't!" I exclaimed.

But it was too late. The one that would make a very good wife for me had already taken the message and was coming over to introduce herself. She took my hand and asked me politely, what my name was? Where I came from? How long I had stayed in Thailand? How old I was?

Oh, but I looked so young! Then, out of words and wisdom, she stood and looked at the floor, moving her hips slightly, hoping I would say or do something. Which I did.

"Would you like a drink?" I asked.

Her eyes came back and she smiled at me.

"Singha bia" she spoke softly.

I ordered the desired brew and leaned back a little. Jui looked at me longingly and when I smiled back, she took it as an invitation to snuggle up and put an arm around me. She fit so nicely into my embrace, it was like hand in glove. I heard her sigh.

"What is it?" I asked.

She shook her head.

"So now you're sabai (comfortable)?"

"Yes" I heard her say "very much sabai."

And she planted a kiss on my neck.

So I took fair Jui out for a nightly stroll. It had been a while since I had walked the streets of Pakarang hand in hand with an Isaan girl. We looked at the boutiques and street front vendors. I bought Jui a T-shirt that read *Yes they are. No you can't!*

Of course she had no clue as to what it meant. But that didn't matter. Everybody was walking around with T-shirts with no knowledge at all what was printed on their chests.

Of course we had to stop and eat something.

After all, this was Thailand. Jui had one of those hard, leathery dinosaur-skins they call blah meuk (squid). I guess they don't have these in Isaan, in the middle of dry land.

I took her down to the beach. A short distance from the sounds and sights of bustling Soi Bangla the waves rolled in with a soothing heartbeat frequency. We found a bench and sat there for a while, listening to the Andaman waves gently lapping at the white sand and the wind shushing the palm trees. It was a full-moon night. Again.

I don't know, somehow I always had the feeling that on Phuket, you have a full moon every week or so. Every time I look up, there it is - big and round and shiny! Back home we didn't have so many full moons. Maybe it was the clouds...

"Does your country have a moon, too?" Jui asked.

"Yes" I said "every country in the world has a moon!"

"Every country?"

Jui seemed surprised. Wow, how many countries were there?

"Oh, I don't know" I answered "hundreds, for sure?"

"Are you joking me?"

Jui looked me straight in the eye.

"I know Thailand and Farang, Burma, and Laos. And Jippun (Japan)."

I said "I am not sure exactly how many countries there are, but there are certainly more than that. In Europe alone there are have more than forty and in the US there are 52 states."

"And all of them have a moon?"

"Yes" I said "but it is really the same moon everywhere, you see!"

Now Jui knew that I was bullshitting her. No way for one moon to shine in all these places at the same time! I insisted for a while, pointing out that the earth was round and that the moon was more or less shining on half of its nightly surface all the time. But Jui was having none of it. Finally - as not to make her mad - I gave in and conceded that the earth had many moons. Roughly one for each country. Most countries had a moon for themselves, but the poorer ones had to share. The next question was, obviously, which countries had more than one moon?

I drew foolish little Jui close and gave her a kiss.

"Do you want to fly to the moon with me?" I asked.

"Wow!" she exclaimed "I never knew one can go there? Can we go today? Are there people up there? How do we get there, with a long-tail boat? With an airplane?"

"No" I said "we'll take a Suzi."

"Now I know you bullshit me again" Dukdah said.

"Actually not" I replied "Let's go to the Rasta Bar and I'll show you my big old Suzi."

It was one of those magic nights. Once in a while in steamy Pakarang it is like that, you know. For some un-known reason Phuket has those special nights. Nothing is planned, everything happens by pure incident. Sud-denly the air is fresh with a fragrance of jasmine. Everybody is in a good mood, everybody smiles and there is even a parking space to be had on Soi Bangla.

Jui placed her sweet behind on the pillion of the Intruder and sat like an angel. Thai girls seem to be born with this ability to go with the beat of a motorbike. Maybe it is because they start to ride on a bike in their mother's womb.

Slowly and heavily we trucked onto 200 Phi Road.

It was a dark night, only a few stars twinkled in the black sky - except, of course, a cloud drew back and there was the brightly shining full moon above the mountains, as always beaming benignly down at earth. After we passed the Simon-Cabaret curve I let power loose. The Suzi's husky grumble turned into a full-fledged roar as she took on the mountain.

Right into the full moon we rode, like something out of a Jules Verne novel or a Spielberg movie.

I am sure Jui sensed it too, even though it lasted only a couple of minutes. A sense of being lifted and born by a flying Suzuki chopper, riding through the dark and un-known land of people into the realm of Gods.

I barely, barely contained power and hit the breaks in the nick of time. There, on top of the hill, was the Safari; a living, burning, resounding place. A peculiar mix. A little Mad Max, a lot of Swinging Safari and some Gothic Rock, the Safari had all its own style. Parking the bike and walking up the entrance with fair Jui by my side I felt like Indiana Jones - if it wasn't for the hat and the whip.

Jui squeezed my hand and said: "This is not the moon, you know. This is Safari!"

"Yes, I know" I said "We'll make it the moon next time, okay?"

"It doesn't matter" she smiled and her dimples showed. "I knew all the time that you were only joking. But is okay. Do you want to dance with me?"

I certainly would! Jui let me drag her tender body close to mine and from this moment on, when we stood as two people who had become one, the music changed. Gone were the slashing drums and the pounding techno rhythms. Jui and I floated on cellos and violins played by heavenly hands.

But alas. Nothing lasts forever, not even Cinderella could extent the spell of magic till after midnight. After floating around in the air amongst strings and bows, I got kind of thirsty. I knew Jui wanted a Singha beer and I decided to have one, too. At the bar I met somebody, I hadn't seen for years.

"Shanoo!"

"Harry!"

Now that was a surprise! The last time I had seen my buddy Shanoo was on a rooftop in Afghanistan, clinging to his machine-gun, only seconds before the house was coming down. We were taking heavy shelling and it was all anarchy. When the roof finally crashed, I lost my conscience. Later I awoke in a small rocky village with a young hijabi woman bending over me, but that's another story. I had never expected to see Shanoo again. Now he showed up in the Safari, of all places.

"Shanoo" I said "how did you get out of that mess?"

He grinned and said: "Nothing much to tell. I was lucky I got nothing broken by the fall, so I decided to take it easy for a while..."

It turned out that Shanoo was working in Phuket town as a medical. So we sat there, shooting the bull for a while, until I felt a tuck on the arm.

"Christ" I exclaimed "I forgot about Jui!"

I introduced her to Shanoo and he said "Don't I know you from somewhere?"

He scratched his head.

"Yes" he finally said "you were the one with the money bundle in your stomach!"

Jui reddened and nodded her head.

"Tell me the story" I asked.

"No" Jui said.

Then, thoughtfully she added: "I angry my boyfriend and I eat all his monee..."

"You can't eat money" Shanoo interrupted.

"Can!" Jui insisted with a mocking face that made her look like an angry cat.

"Eat monee can! Eat love cannot!"

"At least not without getting it surgically removed" Shanoo replied.

I wondered... what did he do with the money after he had removed it surgically, but I forgot to ask.

I don't know about you, but I don't meet old buddies who have risen from the dead very often. So I invited Shanoo to go with us and find a place, where we would be able to talk some more. As it turned out, he would rather rock and roll. To reminiscence the old days, I suggested Rio Bravo.

Down at Rio Bravo it was Creedence Clearwater time, which suited us fine. This was the music we used to fire our adrenaline on, when we were young and did what young men had to do.

"Do you still drink Jack Daniel's?" Shanoo asked.

I admitted that I did. So we ordered a bottle and when it was gone, we ordered another one.

Soi Bangla was having one of its special nights - what with fragrance of jasmine and smiles and even an available parking space - and we were having a ball. The whole house was singing along to Bad Moon Rising. At one time we discussed whether each other still could make a hundred and I recall Shanoo on the floor with two girls sitting on his back, doing push-ups.

Suddenly it wasn't Rio Bravo any more and it wasn't Creedence any more either. The moon had gone and the first rays of a rising sun were sending silver-plated darts into the air. My eyes hurt and I squeezed them shut while slipping back into the realms of dreams.

A few hours later I awoke again and decided to get up, since I had to go to the toilet.

To my surprise, I found six people in the room next to me. Shanoo was there, Jui and four other girls, a couple of which looked suspiciously like ladyboys. I supposed we must have had a ball last night...

Upon returning from the bathroom, I found that Shanoo had awakened, too.

"Man" he said "you sure as hell got my head spinning with that whisky of yours!"

He looked at Jui, heavily snoring away in her sleep.

"She reminds me of somebody we used to know, hmm..."

He scratched his head.

"I think her name was Trong or Trink..."

"Trang" I said.

"Right" said Shanoo "She also could do things with her body."

He bowed down and kissed Jui on the nose. Jui cuddled up close to him.

"Teerak!" I heard her whisper gently.

Well. Still I had my chopper waiting outside. In case anybody else wanted me to fly her to the moon...

Little Miss Sao

You are not handsome, she noted, but I will go with you anyway. Where is your motobike?

Soi Seadragon has always been a favourite of mine. It was an amazing thing this horse-shoe shaped soi, built for pleasure only. I have been sitting in those bars off and on for years, in steamy hot and splashing wet nights and at any time of day. Soi Seadragon is a metaphor of life. People come and go. Everybody has a different story to tell, everybody makes different experiences here. Yet, when seen from a distance, Soi Seadragon remains the same. It beats to the pulse of life. Sleeps through the morning, opens in the late afternoon, rambles through the night. Every day the same schedule. Always the girls. Always the farangs. Always the laughter. Always too hot. Never seems to change.

I made a sport out of visiting each of all the bars at least once. The interesting thing is - you might think they are all the same. Loud music, barstools, hammers and nails. But that is not so. Every bar has a different ambience, a different feel, no matter how. The bars are like families. Every family has its ways and mores. And every family likes to think they are different. And they are.

Go to the Drinks and Dreams, for instance. In spite of all the fun and noise, you will be able to sit in an old English sofa under the picture of Big Ben and read a genuine book, while the vivid adwhoreable Pakarang highlife rotates around you.

Or take the Sexy No. Nine Bar at the bottom of Soi Seadragon. This bar has the double advantage of ena-bling you to see the swinging buttocks of the dancers in the Lipstick A Go Go through the open doors... besides enjoying the presence of dames a plenty by your elbows. And then there is the High Seasons Bar. I am not supposed to tell you this, but if you pass the little entrance beside the fake fireplace you will enter a little backdoor speakeasy, where you are in for a special treat. Here my discreetness kicks in - but go see for yourself!

One night as I was doing my rounds, I noticed that the Sweetheart Bar had a hundred balloons as well as flowers, signs and food displayed. Treading closer, I could read the text on a banner: *Happy wedding Rainbow*.

It was only six o'clock in the evening, far too early for any serious action. But in contrast to the others the Sweetheart Bar was already half filled. I took a seat and was immediately greeted by three ladies who fought each other to accommodate me with cold refreshment towels, flowers, food and drink. As I hadn't been out all week, I was in the mood for a little hanky-panky. So when one of the lovely ladies placed her shapely behind in my lap I happily gave her a kiss on the neck. She smelled of lime fruit and Sunsilk shampoo.

"One drink for me?" she asked and gave me her hand. It was dry and warm, very inviting.

"My name Noi. What your name?"

I told her.

"You want some to eat? Sao has marry today, so food is for free."

By the way - where was lucky Sao anyway?

"Ah" Noi said "Sao will be here soon. She and her husband come here seven o'clock."

And so they did. At seven sharp (farang time!) an open jeep drove up the narrow entrance to the bar. The car was covered with garlands, flowers and fake money bills.

Out stepped the proud groom and the happy bride. There was something familiar about the woman. I took a second look... yes! Pictures emerged in my mind. Fond pictures.

Actually I remembered little Miss Sao very well from a time before her marriage. Her original Thai name was Fah Rorng (thunder). And thunderous she was, even though... She was such a small thing, you know, maybe just about 145 centimetres in pumps. All legs and ass, not much of a bosom. So she made up for it by making a point out of wearing ultra-diminutive shorts and ultra-high heels; a combination that showed off her awesome thighs and firm glutei.

In addition, Sao knew that farang people go wild for the warm, deep tan that Thai girls obtain so easily. She made a routine out of spending a little time at the beach most days. As a result, her skin was radiating a warm, bronze sensuality. She had always been the first choice of the newcomers. As the psalmist put it "her cup was running over", and I mean in every sense of the word. Sao was wild. Even in low season, at times where the rains flooded the pavements and nobody but kiniau (stingy) Italians with garlic breath roamed the streets she was still able to dig up young, slim, blond Swedes with long noses and money in their wallets. She never slept alone.

I have had the good fortune of spending a whole month with Sao. And I didn't have to pay for her services, either. Why...?

I just happened to be there when she needed a friend. Not any friend, but somebody who could listen, understand and give an opinion. She had many Thai girlfriends, of course. But, you know, in Thailand... when you are happy, you have lots of friends. But when you are unhappy, you cry alone. Sao had lots of European friends, too. But they all stayed overseas. She was working them in a schedule, so that only one of her worshippers at a time was staying on Phuket for holiday. It was not the money either, Sao had plenty. Most of the time she enjoyed taking me out and paying bills herself. At that particular time, Sao was sad and nobody was there to comfort her. She had the low season blues.

Originally I had met her at a local temple. She was seeking the advice of the abbot. Not surprisingly, he told her to do merit and eat vegetables. I watched her kneeling and patting the floor three times with the palms of her hands. When she rose and turned around, the two of us were looking straight into each other's eyes. Her melting gaze was so open that I had a hard time standing up for it and keeping my eyes steady. Slowly and tantalisingly she extended a slender hand, never failing to look me in the eyes.

Holding my fingers she said in a husky voice: "Where do you go, farang? Can I go with you?"

I felt a prickle down my spine as if somebody had put an ice cube down my neck.

"Yes" I answered "you can go with me. And I am going where ever you want me to go!"

Sao looked me over even more closely.

"You are not handsome" she noted "but I will go with you anyway. Where is your motobike?"

As the proud groom and Sao, the happy bride, jumped off the jeep, she recognized me at once. She tried to hide it, but I could tell by that little hesitating twist of her head that she had seen me and not yet had made her mind up whether or how to react. First thing it was important to keep face and draw the blinds. Naive and trustful, as most tourist farangs were, her spouse might not even know the true nature of little Sao's business. But it took only a few minutes for her to adjust and make a stand. All smiles she dragged her proud husband - a young Swedish looking man - and introduced us. With a discreet wink she presented me as an old farang friend who was married to a Thai friend and who had helped her translating some important English papers.

What audaciousness?

No, not at all. Farangs were easy and at this phase her Swedish newlywed would believe everything she said. One often heard farang-phrase in Thailand was "I believe my wife". When a man said that, you and everybody else except for the guy himself knew he was being goofballed by the book.

Sao even let go of her spouse - who's name was Eric by the way - and seated her gorgeous legs next to me.

"Teerak" she whispered in my ear and even through the whispering her erotic huskiness sounded through like a promise "I never forget you. I can go with you for a short time if you want to. I just have to be careful that my husband or his friends won't know about this. Can you meet me at midnight at the Vienna Bar?"

She smiled that wonderfully open and trustworthy smile that Thai girls give you when they are double dealing and beguiling somebody's head off. She looked so glorious. I envied Eric, who was lucky enough to carry little Miss Sao - Miss Thunder - up and away. But I also felt sorry for him for being such a cuckoo.

A short-time with lovely Sao in heat surely would have made my day. Except that I could not be sure of what little Sao really had in mind. It might be a sweet short-time for old-time's sake. But it might as well be an attack by a hired friend with a baseball bat. So I did what a man has to do. I made an appointment with gorgeous Sao at Vienna Bar at midnight.

But I didn't go there. I had a drink with Stephen at the entrance of the Rock Hard instead, trying to make up my mind whether to go upstairs or stay downstairs. You know the rest of the story.

Another night in paradise

Even - God forbid - the girls!

Every time I've been away from Phuket for more than a few days I promise myself - when I come back, I'm never going to leave the island again. Especially when the journey takes me north to colder pastures, pictures of warm, lush, succulent Phuket with green palm trees, white beaches and blue waters immediately spring to mind and I miss my tropical home even as the airplane touches wintery ground.

But still... you know how it is, once in a while, after a long while, you feel the urge to go somewhere else. Breathe different air, see different people, hear different sounds. Man is so built, one doesn't appreciate what's right under one's nose. Even paradise begins to bore you, if you stay there long enough. You get fed up with the food, the people, the landscape. Even - God forbid - the girls. After a while, the food becomes too spicy, the people too content, the landscape too green and the girls too greedy. You don't even notice the daily deadly motorbike accidents any more than the mosquitos or the boozed farangs.

"Wouldn't it be nice" you think "to get away from the loud bars, the hot weather and the perpetual *how much you give me's*?"

Your mind conjures up pictures of civilized Westerners, meeting on time, talking sense, operating fax machines and water wells that actually work.

But hey - already at the airport you find out that you were mistaken. Your mind has pulled a trick on you. You had plainly forgotten that the world you once were a part of is full of tasteless food, reckless people, trees without leaves, cold grey skies... and frustrated, self-minded girls the size of elephants but with the sex appeal of herrings.

Oh well. I am not going to waste any more words on the world outside of Phuket. I have been away, it was business, it was pure misery. But now I'm back and so are the happy times.

The first thing I did upon my arrival was to buy myself a new bike. Not quite new of course, you can't buy a new American motorcycle in Thailand, but a second hand one.

I would keep my old Honda Dream, of course. No man in his right mind would do away with his "Mule of Asia" as Stephen called it. My Honda is a good old bike, unbeatable when in downtown traffic. You can put your market-vegetables in the basket up front plus a bottle of Mekhong (not that I ever drink that poisonous contaminant). You can drape bags full of plah meuk (squids) and milk-cartons in plastic bags around the handlebars. You can squeeze a bucket of mangosteen in between your knees. I have been riding my Dream to Soi Bangla and Soi Seadragon so many times that by now this mule knew the way home all by herself.

It is not quite true though that buying a new bike was the first thing I did. The **very** first thing I did, when I stepped out of the plane was, I kissed the runway. I did the Pope.

Go on and laugh! I kissed the bloody asphalt and I didn't give a damn about the stares and snickers of my fellow passengers. Let them see I was doing the Pope, let them ridicule my posture, kneeling with my derriere up in the air.

The important thing was, I had come back to the one and only place where I could have that certain irreplaceable Thai thing they call sanuk (fun). Okay, so I kissed the bloody runway, picked up my bags, took the limo to Pakarang and marched right into Big Bike on Rath U Thit. The garage was filled with motorcycles and parts and grease monkeys and the smell of oil and leather. I marched on into the tiny air-con cubicle where Jay stood erect, issuing orders, directing her troops like a French lieutenant.

I looked Jay right in the eye and said: "I want a Harley and I want it now!"

Jay didn't raise an eyebrow. She has been into motorcycles for decades and she knows the look on a man's face, when the time has come. For those who have never seen Jay's own Harley: she even had a turbo attached to it.

So she showed me the available bikes, I picked one and minutes later I was ready to enjoy Phuket the way it should be done - riding a big bike, enjoying the sound, letting the warm winds caress my face.

It was early afternoon, so I spent a few hours emptying my bags, trying to locate my house-keeper, looking up a friend and taking my new bike for a ride.

If you have been in Pakarang, I guess you are familiar with the road to Kata. It is one of my favourite jaunts for a short ride. I enjoyed the hills and waved at the elephants. I passed the Safari and looked at the oceanside with new eyes. Man, it was good to be back home!

But even riding my new Harley and enjoying the sun and the sky and the palm-trees could not quench that special feeling in my guts. You know what I'm talking about... I just couldn't wait for night to fall and all the action to begin that I had been missing so much while I was away. To shorten the time I took a drink at the Sky Inn. In case you don't know, Sky Inn was a wondrous, bizarre place, even by Pakarang standards in the old days. Some of the apartments there were elegant suites with mahogany furniture and ivory inlays. The high rise had this quaint Swiss restaurant on top with the sleigh and the skier and the woodwork, outrageously built from original imported Swiss fir-parts, and even the freaking deer antlers.

But at the bottom, a universe totally different from the high-browed fir and mahogany closets opened its funky parlours to anybody who was broad-minded enough to enjoy pure, undiluted sanuk. Like the biblical giant with clay feet, Sky Inn towered on sodomite foundations. At ground level one found funky shops, restaurants, beauty parlours etc. that bore no relation to the luxury above. Cracked paint and cheap interior prevailed and gave no clue to the abodes above.

Of course it wasn't Thailand if the opposites didn't meet and mingle in the elevators. Tourists in shorts, business people in designer dresses, Thai managers with mia nois and first of all the kathoeys... they all stood cramped together in a moving tin can for a minute or two. The tourists staring at the kathoeys, the frozen chosen keeping their eyes on the floor, and the kathoeys admiring themselves in the broken mirror, screeching *sawasdee kha* (hello) and *how are you today* at everybody.

I took it all in and had a good time. And sitting with my back to the parking lot (where my newly bought HD was parked!) I had a grand view to a Chinese noodle restaurant, a Thai supermarket and a beauty parlour that was specially geared toward kathoey needs. Suddenly somebody somewhere put on a B.B. King record. The sound of

Lucille hitting them signature notes made my hair stand up. So when one of the ladyboys came over to bid me *sawasdee kha* and ask for a drink, he found a man with emotions. A man who for once did not immediately make it clear that he was strictly and hardcore hetero.

As it turned out, that particular ladyboy had been in Sweden lately, where she had spent several months making love in saunas and Volvo cars.

"Europe is so cold" she said with an all too girlish shrug "I thought I was going to die!"

I laughed and she added: "But they all have big, big bananas, same same!"

He or she glanced at me. I knew what was coming.

"I bet you also have a big banana" the katheoy said invitingly.

I said: "Yes, you bet. And do you know where I and my big banana are going to go tonight?"

I saw a secret smile flicker over her face. Another one down! But that was not going to happen. B.B. King had been replaced by some Thai pop singer who constantly pitched his melody a quarter tone low, making my skin break out with horror bumps.

It was getting dark. I paid my bill and swung one leg over the saddle of my Harley. I was going to go home, park my new chopper and take the good old Honda Dream mule to town. No point in riding bulky, heavy machinery into cramped Pakarang at party time. But then I thought, what the heck, let today be a special occasion!

When I rounded the beach corner and headed up Soi Bangla, I even decided to put on a little show. Why not let everybody know the Fox is back in town!

Down to first gear, crank the mother up and let her ride on one wheel for a moment. The ladies yelled and applauded. Which meant that they took me for a green-horn - real dumb easy spender. I didn't care. To be honest, I enjoyed. I was still in that special "coming home to Phuket" state of mind. And speaking of coming home to Pakarang... I have been around some, I have been a few places. But let me tell you - there ain't nothing like sweet Soi Seadragon in them good old days. I drove around the horse-shoe a couple of times and enjoyed the cries and hollers of the ladies. Jesus, they were so pretty! I had been looking forward to this moment - I had fantasised about the Nings and Nongs and Leks and Saos while in dreary office buildings in Des Moines and sterile hotel rooms in Copenhagen. And even though my fantasies had painted it all golden - when I saw the girls again and this special scent of perfume, flowers and incense once again hit my nose, it took me aghast.

I said to myself: This time, for once, I am going to grab a whole bunch. I am going to take a bar-full of ladies and have a party at my house the whole night long!

I took a few rounds and finally parked the bike at the Buffalo Soldier. My old friend Rhumba the Dreadlock was at the desk, mixing drinks under the giant Bob Marley flag. According to himself the reason they call him Rhumba is that a certain roll of his hips drives the girls wild. But I suspect that the fact he was born on Cuba has something to do with it. The only rolls I had seen on him where the handles under his shirt.

Rhumba flashed his white shark teeth and gave me this droll "hey mahn" Rasta welcome. Two Scandinavian girls hovered by the counter. Rhumba raised an eyebrow, thus indicating that he already had done at least one of them. Funny, how black and white are drawn together, isn't it?

Whenever the topic hits exploitation of poor little Asian girls by fat and sleazy tourists, I use Rhumba and his fellows from the Rasta Bar to illustrate that in Pakarang, at least, there is absolute equality and sisterhood of man. You won't guess the scoring rate of the Rasta boys or how much money they make on Scandinavian girls.

I liked listening to Rhumbas stories once in a while - and actually I felt like drawing out the time before I hit My Love Bar and all the rest. Foreplay, you know :-) So I sat next to the frozen Scandinavian girls and let Rhumba serve me one of his oozy drinks. And while my ears where listening to the narration of Rhumbas latest conquests my eyes were watching the action at Sexy Number Nine Bar where the girls were dancing, hollering and having a good time. As the drinks went down and spread this lazy hazy feeling in my guts I knew it was going to be another great night in Paradise.

Ah, and the Curvaceousness of Rainbow

"I be your wife tonight!" she said.
And smiled.

I had met her a few times. She was one of umpteen free-lancers in the abysmal and migrational pack of she-hounds that populated Pakarang. I had seen her in the bars she "worked", I had seen her with farangs at the Buk Ruk waterfall during the day and at the food stalls at night and I had noticed the shapely curves on her volup-tuous figure... But I had never made her acquaintance. Until the day she literally bumped into me, with her Honda Dream, bringing both of us to the ground. By Thai standards it wasn't really an accident or an injury. Just a little blood and scrape, enough to make you hurt, but not enough to remember.

Still, I took her to the hospital. Rainbow may never have heard of germs and infections, but even though she was the one that had impacted me I felt responsible for at least having her checked and medicated, if required.

The hospital was hot and though there were no patients in line, we had to wait for some time because a pickup truck rode up with a corpse on the cargo area. It wasn't even covered, I could see the blood stained face of a dead man. It didn't look like an accident, more like a shootout. Jokingly the men dragged the body into the hall and let the paramedics handle the matter.

Meanwhile I studied the exhibition row of deformed foetus' in methylate bottles. The zombies made me shudder, but Rainbow pointed and laughed at the hor-rendous alien faces and the distorted bodies as if it was a comic strip.

I didn't really know what this ghastly display was supposed to warn you against, but the condom and AIDs commercial on the side were clear enough. Strangely, even though AIDs commercials were to be found practically everywhere, nobody seemed to prepare. Rather than loosing a call, the girls would accept bareback traffic.

"Does it hurt?" I asked her.

Rainbow puckered her lips and twisted her head.

"No, mai pen rai. Only a little bit."

Finally it was our turn to see the doctor. She gave Rainbow's injuries a quick glance than injected a shot of antibiotics - as they always do. A prescription for painkillers. I paid the bill at the cashier's and that was it.

Rainbow did a mock curtsey and gave me a wai.

"Thank you" she said calmly.

I noticed a moist reflexion in her eye.

"De nada" I said "For what?"

"For taking me to the doctor and paying for my medication. Nobody has ever done that before."

I sensed that Rainbow was really moved. How sweet. I couldn't help but smile.

"Come on" I said "it is nothing really."

Rainbow smiled back, wiping an eye.

"I buy you breakfast, OK?"

Surely it wasn't breakfast time, but a meal and a drink with shapely Rainbow did seem attractive. So I let her pick the place and we headed for Laan Sukapok - the favourite restaurant for Isaan girls. The name of the place is not really Laan Sukapok (the dirty restaurant). We just called it that because this place had no name, even though it may have been the most popular eatery among the Pakarang girls - and because it WAS dirty, even by Thai standards. Just very few tourists there, only the casual backpacker. Too hardcore Isaan, you know. But this place certainly was known by every bar girl, every Thai worker and every expat in the city. Surely besides the native menu the native prices played an important part in the popularity. Where else could you get a full meal, a seat and a table for a meagre twenty Baht?

The Laan Sukapok is completely open to one side, the interior extends to the pavement and as rasping and funky as the place looks and smells on the inside, the view is great, as the very heart and soul of Pakarang street life displays and performs right in front of your eyes.

Rainbow ordered Chinese noodles and a sauce that looked (and smelled) like barf. And even though they do have a few dishes at the Laan Sukapok that might be digestible by farang stomachs, I decided to stick with a drink.

Time runs fast when sitting in Laan Sukapok watching the great entertainment. So suddenly it was early afternoon, time for a hotweather-nap, and I was going to drive Rainbow home. On the bike she put her soft arms around me and leaned her head against my shoulder. Then, at her doorstep, she asked me inside.

"Come take a sleep with me" she said "No bumsing, just sleeping a little bit..."

I wonder if any man could lie next to Rainbow's curves and not be fired up by zest. But even though I did resist temptation, Rainbow could not. The presence of a white-skinned farang in her bed and coy thankfulness in her veins caused her system to flush various places, I guess. While we were "sleeping" several other girls entered the house. Nobody took much notice of me. After all, catching farangs is the name of the game in Pa-karang. But as the noise level rose, sleeping became impossible. Already the girls were warming up to the evening.

Was it party time? Of course! Every night in Pakarang was party time. Putting on makeup, watching them-selves in broken mirrors, trying on different clothes the girls had a ball in hopeful anticipation of the catch the night would bring. One of the girls fetched Mekhong whisky, manau and coke, and of course Rainbow and I were invited to join. It was expected that Rainbow too, would go through the motions and get ready for her nocturnal stint, but Rainbow, still thankful, whispered in my ears: "Teerak, please you can have a short-time for free."

Sitting on the floor in her sarong among the other girls I once again realised just how pretty and well rounded she was. There she sat, au naturel, wearing no makeup, no fancy clothes, barefoot, among all those outrageous girls dressed to kill and made up to tease... looking heartbreakingly lovely with that pneumatic body of hers, all apple pie and mama's chicken soup. As she shifted her curves into another position and let a luscious hip shine through the garment I became aware that she wore no briefs. But that was nothing unusual. Thai girls love their bras, I doubt if you will ever see a female Thai person without her bra regardless where or when. But panties...

The bliss of an amorous tete a tete with fair Rainbow sounded really promising but somehow the sight of nat-ural Rainbow even in her curvaceousness and panty-lessness did not only arouse me, but made me a little...

sad. She so much embodied Madonna and Babylon Sister in the same person that oozed heart-breaking and compelling vulnerability. She was a lost lone lovebird in a safe and familiar cage with an open door that for some reason could not be trespassed.

Sad? I pondered my feelings. Even after all these years among calculative and manipulative women that could give you one or two great nights as Stephen put it - and, if you stuck with one of them, years of gruelling and viperish torments - was I still a romantic?

"Would you like to go out with me tonight?" I asked Rainbow.

"Yes teerak!" she beamed, sat up and reached for her makeup set "Let's go dance!"

I made it clear that I did not want her to make up and dress the sophenee (working girl) part. It would be nice for once to pretend we were an ordinary couple.

It took a while for Rainbow to let the idea sink in. But then she laughed and placed her head in my lap, looking up at me with those inscrutable dark almond eyes. As I stroke her pitch black hair she said "I be your wife tonight!" and smiled.

No, we did not go dancing. It so happened that a movie band visited Pakarang that night. We rode up the steep hill to the platform where they had erected a big outdoor screen and parked an old truck with an ancient but vicious carbon arc lamp hurtling its screamingly brilliant rays like hot spears through the side and on to the silver screen. The heat from the carbon rod disgorged a snarling fume and the diesel generator coughingly added to it with its exhaust.

A crowd of spectators - all Thai - had gathered, most of them perched on their Honda Dreams. Rainbow and I sat leaning against each other in the warm tropical night while Chinese swordsmen and swordswomen flew up walls and over rooftops, darting battle disks and spewing light rays from their eyes. I brought out a Bia Chang and a spritzer that we had retailed at Seven Eleven along with some prawn crackers. The full moon barely managed to shine against the lights of the movie, but it was there.

Time went by slowly and blissfully. I sat and enjoyed intoxication - not only by alcohol, but by the magic of it all. The lush night, the blessed oblivion... but most of all, Rainbow's sweet nearness and fragrance. Everybody was watching the events on the screen. Once in a while I felt Rainbows gentle elbow nudging my ribs, when she saw something funny or exciting. But I must admit I was not looking at the movie much. I looked at my "wife" Rainbow.

At one time she noticed I was watching her. Coyly she took my hand and planted a kiss on the back of my fingers.

"Teerak...." she whispered.

I opened my mouth, but quickly Rainbow placed her palm over my lips. I knew that she knew what I was going to say.

"Don't speak" she said softly.

And through the dark and through her smile I saw a moist reflexion in her eye.

Navy Day

Every bar girl would now shift into emergency mode.

"Tonight I go with a farang from Saweden (Sweden)" Lek beamed "and he give me two thousand Baht".
Laughingly she waved some bills in my face.
"Come, I pay for beer!"
It was six o'clock in the morning. It was dark. I was still in bed. Lek was drunk. I didn't feel like having a beer at all.
"Why are you here then?" I asked her.
Lek's answer wasn't clear, but apparently she had left her one night stand sleeping in his hotel for a time-out and had planned to go back to him later.
I loved Lek. Like a sister that is. We had never had any sexual bonds, neither had any of us wanted to. I had helped her financially at a time where she was really down and out and in return - being a Thai person and holding all appropriate civil rights - she had facilitated life for me on several occasions. Finally, just a month ago, she had moved in with me and the other three ladies that lived in my house.
"Listen Lek" I said "I think you should go back to your boyfriend and have some sleep. Or give him what he paid you for..."
"Okay..." she said hesitatingly and sat down on the bed, tucking up her legs. I waited for a minute, knowing what was going to happen. And yes, Lek's head began to sag more and more and a few moments later she was sound asleep. I pulled a blanket over her body and went back to sleep myself.
Peace didn't last long, though. Slamming doors, noisy laughter... my other three housemates were coming

back from town as a bunch. You might think they would go to sleep, but that goes to prove you are not Thai. What they did, they fired up in the kitchen. Eating time!

Not that the racket disrupted Lek's sleep. But I decided that I might as well rise and shine.

In the kitchen the girls were all aglow with great news. As soon as she spotted me Ning shouted: "Navy comes to town!"

In case you don't grasp the intricate ramifications of the event (which would be comprehensible), "US Navy coming to town" was something like a war cry. Every bar girl would now shift into emergency mode. As long as the handsome, wealthy, and well endowed warriors from across the pond were going to stay in Pakarang you might as well consider all previously existing agreements with any bar girl cancelled. The girls would throw themselves at the friendly fire, working overtime to wallow in love, sex, and sweet excess.

Lek appeared at the door. So our noise had awakened her all the same. But the Navy news was no novelty to her. Instead she had news for us.

"I know" she mumbled blearily "But do you know they have put Noi in monkey house?"

Noi was one of our old friends. According to Lek the police had caught Noi and her boy-friend allegedly with a joint in the boy-friends room. Both of them were put in jail for drug infringement because the boyfriend had claimed that Noi too had smoked the weed. But Noi never touched the stuff, everybody knew that. The farang had paid his way out of jail, but Noi... If she could not raise bail - thirty thousand, how could she? - would risk a long confinement, maybe a year or more! I made myself a drink.

In this world people disappeared all the time. Some went to jail simply because the police wanted money. Others were shot by enemies or business partners or knifed by ex-lovers. A lot of people died in motorbike accidents, careless and stupid tourists died in the water currents off Kata Beach. And some people just moved.

But Ning was not going to let it be. She decided we should bail Noi out. She was going to make a collection. Already she was counting on her fingers. The four girls and Harry, that made five. The twelve or so girls from My Love Bar, that made seventeen...

"Harry" she said "if we are twenty, how much for each?"

"Fifteen hundred" I replied.

"Oh" she replied as disappointment showed on her face.

"But Harry, you are farang" she accused me "you must to pay more!"

Sure, I didn't mind helping an old friend. And I knew the iron clad rule "farangs must pay (more)". But briefly I wondered whether it would stop there. As I said, people disappeared all the time and my resources were limited. I couldn't help them all.

As you may guess, at the end I put up most of the money, Ning handled the formal and informal affairs and finally all five of us drove up to the monkey house in a rented jeep. Even so, negotiations took most of the afternoon, so I spent the time with my laptop and a cool drink at a food stall next to the jail entrance until finally they let Noi out. She was shaken but kept her posture. She waied all of us with her hands up over her nose then she kneeled down in front of me and positioned her forehand and palms on the ground.

"Come on" I said a little embarrassed "Noi that's okay. Maybe you will have to help me out some other time."

Noi rose, embraced me and planted quick kisses on my cheeks.

"I never forget!" she promised.

We celebrated Noi's new freedom at the Sala Isaan. In case you don't know, Isaan is a rather big and poor rural geographic part of Eastern Thailand that supplies the richer parts of the country - among them Phuket of course - not only with rice, but even with a steady stream of emigrant workforces. Gaew, Ning and Lek were all born and raised in small villages amongst rice paddies. And so the music of Isaan has spread to the rest of the country with them. Actually you could say that Isaan music was the soul music of Thai people. It was aired on the radio and on the TV and it was being constantly played in the numerous karaoke bars - accompanied by videos that showed beautiful, white-skinned girls with nose jobs in waterfalls, who could not help but undress down to bikinis or even less. The girls, not the waterfalls.

At the Sala Isaan Thai people met to party and make sanuk according to their own local dance rites which seemed mostly to consist of slow ballet like movements with raised elbows and spread fingers.

We had a ball and I enjoyed the girls' country dancing. Of course they wanted me to dance along with them as there is nothing funnier for a Thai person than to see a farang make a fool of himself while "dancing" to Isaan music.

"What you know Isaan music?" Gaew asked me.

"I think I do" I replied "Mostly pentatonic scale. Basically only in one mode without real chords or changes. Beat is always four to the bar with emphasis on three and four..."

Gaew laughed out loud. "Harry teerak, you understand no thing. Isaan music is for the heart, it makes you happy. It is sad text, but when you dance, you are laughing."
"You are right" I smiled "that is a much better definition."

After an hour or so we left the Isaan dancery and proceeded to the My Love Bar as business had to be taken care of. And since business consisted of sitting at the bar, flirting with farangs, business was also sanuk and therefore indispensable.

That night boss Somchai made our drinks on the house. Which I deemed no less than justified. After all he had his bargirl back - and Noi was not a bad earner for him - without spending a single Baht.

It was a great Pakarang night, motorbikes and girls everywhere. The bikes flashing in neon and the girls swarming like exotic humming birds all around. Earrings, skirts, high heels, twerking butts, juggling chests.

Noi touched my arm.

"I have no boy-friend tonight and I don't like sleeping alone. You know I am afraid of phee (ghosts)."

She lightened up a smile to rival a Christmas tree.

"Will you sleep with me tonight?"

"Noi, there really are no phees to be afraid of..." I began. The Christmas tree went out. She placed a hand over my lips.

"No!" she begged "I want to go with you, okay? You have good heart! You got me out of monkey house! I come for free!"

I shook my head. "Noi, you don't have to pay me back. But if you insist I am sure there will be other occasions, where I would call your help. And helping or paying back doesn't necessarily include sex."

Noi looked at me in bewilderment. Her eyebrows twitching.

"Why don't you like me? Am I not sexy like farang girls? Look, I made my hair today and my fingers..."

She showed me her self-luminous nails. Her eyes looked into mine. They were very dark and very pretty.

"Are you hungry?" I asked "What about a chicken wing?"

"No, I eat already! Where you go? I go with you, okay?"

Finally Noi scowled as she understood that she had to accept my decision. An elderly gentleman with a beard and gold rimmed glasses next to her gave her a smile and she smiled back ostentatiously, indicating that if I didn't want to go with her, she would throw herself at the next idiot that looked her way.

Well, that was fine with me. Go girl! Make some money!

My gaze followed Noi's as she trudged away with her pickup courageously, showing off her butt, waving a naughty backhanded finger at me. Good luck girl and good business!

With Noi gone, I relaxed and enjoyed the scenery. Two of my little house-mates had left with farangs, but Lek and Ning still remained. They were in high spirits and the three of us sang along to "we will, we will *beep* you".

When the bar closed, Lek and I joined the streaming masses up to Lan Sukapok where Lek had a bowl of mee jinn noodle before she left for the Banana to make a pickup.

For once even Stephen was there, he had dropped in for a beer and we talked about girls the expat way. Steven and I had different tastes it seemed, but we agreed on one thing: with the stunners, sex was a bore.

"They don't even try"! Steven said "They are so damn blasé."

I didn't agree though. I mean yes, most stunners are blasé, simply because the guys worship them like saints no matter what. But why should the fact that they were widely admired make them boring in bed? I suspected there must be another explanation. But I had no clue as to what.

The next day was Navy Day. It had been a hot night and even the morning was hot already. I got up and took a shower. Lek and Ning had slept at home, Lek had taken her pickup from the "trap" to our house and Ning had made it back to her room late at night after a short-time at Holiday Inn.

Finally Gaew and Paht wandered in at early afternoon and we prepared for a shared meal. The girls were all excellent cooks, Ning had even managed a food stall back in Isaan. Accordingly, food in our house was always great. Another great thing about the food in our house was that I never was on roll, since I was both man and farang. One of the few advantages: farang always has to pay, but he never has to prepare food... or wash dishes... or do the laundry... all of which by the way, done by hand.

The six of us sat down on the patio floor enjoying the shade and the garden breeze. Gaew had brought a newspaper and she read some of the news to me before using it as a table mat. I was informed that there had been several motorbike accidents that night, sewage from a big hotel had poured out into the sea, and a young bar girl had been murdered by a farang. In Bangkok a young girl had committed suicide by drinking pesticide in her cell to prevent herself from being molested by the police.

We commented on the murder. Though people disappeared and died in motorbike accidents all the time and killings were a common way of dealing with unpleasant business partners and unfaithful husbands, the murder of a bargirl was an extraordinary event. Pakarang's night life had always been flamboyant, but safe.

The girls were uneasy, for the first time I sensed that they were having fearful thoughts about their working conditions.

But as soon as we had finished our generous meal the mood changed. It was Navy Day, remember? After a nap, the girls came together in our living room and began to groom and make up. Lek had sent her pickup away, though the guy was quite handsome and seemed ready to lose some money. Sorry, but ain't nothing beats them Navy strappers!

Enraptured, Gaew, Paht and Lek left early, they weren't going to miss a moment of the party.

Ning and I sat on the veranda, watching the steaming mountains.

"Have you ever been abroad?" I asked her.

"Yes, farang took me to Switzerland once. It was very cold. He made me wear much clothes and a hat, and gloves."

"It must have been in the winter then."

"I don't know, but there was snow everywhere and ice on the water and sharp ice hanging from the roof like a knife..."

She shuddered. I heard a door slamming and saw Boomer, our farang neighbour leave his house and hop on his bike. A few moments' later Dah, his Thai wife came out to lament. For three years she had been with her unfaithful husband, a "butterfly", a Don Juan, a Casanova, who didn't care and didn't mind that everybody knew he was making a cuckquean of his wife. It was not only the money. Poor Dah really loved that old son of a bitch.

The sky was clear, the sun was quickly setting, soon a rosy and reddish glowing band of skies would lighten up behind the mountains of Kathu for a short while before making space for a pale moon.

"Why is he doing this to me?" Dah sobbed as she had done so often.

"I always was a true wife. Yes I make a little work, but only because he gives me so small money!"

Her tears began to roll.

"I know he has other lady, but I don't care if he comes home every night!"

"You should go working while there still is time and you are young" Ning replied "Boomer treats you like a dog."

Dah took a sip of Thai whisky.

"I think of the future all the time. I am already thirty soon, too old to work farangs. Who want go with an old lady?"

She shook the ice in her drink fretfully.

"Dah" I said smilingly "if you ever work farangs, I will be your first customer!"

"Thank you Harry. You want some whisky?"

Traffic was picking up, the road at the bottom of the hill was aflow with motorbikes. The procession of Navy girls in short dresses and high heels had begun. Time for Ning to join the show. I offered her a ride as I was going to watch the show myself.

Downtown at the My Love Bar Lek sat puffing into the whistle I had given her for her birthday, letting out fierce catcalls every time a yummy soldier ambled by.

"Come and *beep* me! I'm so horny!" she yelled.

Ning snorted. "You make noise!" she complained.

And she was right, even through the roar of the speakers Lek's train whistle was a sharp assault on the ears.

I saw Gaew and Paht sitting on their stools. But one chair was vacant.

"Where is Noi?"

"I think she have boyfriend."

"That early?" I asked.

Lek shrugged.

Maybe a short-time. Maybe Noi would arrive later. But Noi never showed up...

The turmoil and noise picked up as more and more marines roamed the streets. Girls hollered and rejoiced as horny marines caressed them and lifted them up in the air like basketballs.

That night was a long and hot one, and the atmosphere was filled with noise, smells, evaporating perfumes and hormones. I guess for the girls it was like Christmas and Easter at the same time. Tonight I was going to take it easy, have a few drinks and spend the rest of the night in front of my computer.

The next morning was calm and the house was empty as all my friends were "working" marines. The verdant hill behind the house oozed peaceful misty morning dew into the scalding glimmering air. It was too hot to sit at home or at a road-stall kitchen. I decided to imbibe my breakfast in the air-conditioned lobby of the Sabai Hotel. I ordered continental breakfast and enjoyed the luxury of freshly squeezed mango juice. The (English speaking) newspaper told the story of the American battleship that was gracing us with its visit and had more details on the bar girl killing. Her identity had been determined as one

Miss Suthapa Nianthar - but I will spare the reader the details of the slaughter, just a hint: unlucky Miss Nianthar had the bad fate of meeting a surgeon on her last assignment, it seemed.

"Miss Nianthar who worked at a Pakarang bar as a cashier leaves a child..."

I kept myself busy writing and reading for the next couple of days. The house was tranquil and I enjoyed the peace as the girls were busy on their Navy stints. Stephen popped in and we chatted for a while. We discussed the Navy's visit and the fracas it had brought along.

"When I first came to Thailand I had no idea how hot-blooded these girls are by nature" Stephen mused "Today I understand a little bit more. Still it is hard to grasp the vehemence with which these Valkyries chase the Navy."

"It is the big S" I said "You know the three big S' that rule the Thai way of life: as in SUAY (handsomeness) and SADANG (money) and SANUK (fun). Thai girls are shackled by emotion and under the spell of love potion no. nine when the mighty warriors of the high West come down to earth in their vessel and uniform..."

"Yes" Stephen added "it is kind of funny though, people always accusing men of being chauvinist swines, picking beautiful young girls for fornication... they should experience the shock of seeing our local girls at a time like this..."

He laughed. "And it even is just one big game. The girls and the navy boys have a heck of the time, buggering each other to kingdom come..."

Then ponderously he added: "And luckily what happened to your poor friend is just a very seldom thing..."

"What do you mean by my poor friend?" I asked perplexed.

"I mean Noi of course" Stephen said "What happened to her is an absolute abnormality in this place. Thank God."

Seeing my stupefied face he added: "I thought you knew her, wasn't she one of your girls?"

"Yes, Noi is a friend of ours. What do you imply saying something *happened to her*?"

"You mean you don't know? Haven't you heard?" Stephen asked back unbelievingly.

Slowly a bad feeling crept into my guts.

"It was all over the news" Stephen said, quoting the newspaper "Miss Nianthar worked at the My Love Bar and she leaves a daughter…"

Instantly I hoped that Stephen was wrong. I rushed down to the My Love Bar. It was open, but only a few of the girls were warming their stools. I noticed that the flags were hanging low and there were black balloons. So Stephen had been right…

There was Gaew, sitting with her pickup - a black marine double her size. As she saw me, she hurried over to hug me and I felt her moist cheek against mine. She held my hand for a minute.

Finally I asked: "What was Noi's real name?"

"Her First Name Suthapa" Gaew said "last name Nianthar. Why?"

It took me a long time and a lot of Jack Daniel's to summon the strength to look the truth in the eye. And I cursed the day I had turned Noi down. I accused myself heavily for letting her go with the bearded killer-surgeon and saying a dumb thing like *what about a chicken wing* instead of saving her life by saying "Yes I go with you".

The Golden Hour of Laan Sukapok

Place with no name everybody knows

If you have stayed in Pakarang for more than the average two to three weeks, you might have noticed this place. Certainly every expat knows it.

I'm talking about the Thai eatery located on the corner of Rath U Thit and Bangla, facing the Hard Rock. The most prominent features of the place are its opening hours. I have never seen it closed except once, on the King's birthday - which made a deep impression on me. I know that the King is like God to Thai people, but closing down the Thai eatery on the corner of Rath U Thit and Bangla is something else.

What's funny is - if the darn place has a name, I never met anybody who knew it. People have to euphemise, saying they are going to "that place which is open all the time" or something to that respect. Maybe it doesn't need a name because every Thai body knows it anyhow. To Thai palates it produces the best down home soul food south of Isaan, you see. On the other hand, if you consider the many names Thai people put on persons and places they know and like, you couldn't understand why an omnipresent topic like this should go unnamed. It's just one of those Thai things I guess.

The most popular of dishes at the unnamed eatery is mee jinn, Chinese noodles. They come with spicy Phuket style sauce that makes them smell like barf and a plate of tua and tua ngo - beans and soy sprouts. I myself do not enjoy eating at this place, I must admit. It is too darn dirty. I mean, sure - living in South East Asia cannot be endeavoured without accepting a little dirt and other natural phenomena. But it doesn't wet me appetite to see lizards, cockroaches, rabies dogs and in the rainy season frogs chase each other under the tables. The single toilet is a horror even to Thai standards. As I said, to Western eyes the mee jinn looks more like barf than anything else. And the stench...

My later wife used to call the place "Laan Sukapok" (the Dirty Shop) and finally that became the nickname to stay with it.

But well, to me it doesn't matter much, you see, because I don't eat there. I just have a shandy, a bia Chang mixed with tonic - they don't have Jack Daniel's, only Mekhong - and use my eyes. I do not use my eyes on the cockroaches. I do not see the rusty oilcans or the rotting piles of garbage on the street in front of the shop. I don't even perceive the eggshells on the floor. What I do is, I enjoy looking at the show.

There is no show, of course. Just real life. 24 hours a day, 7 days a week the Laan Sukapok entertains its visitors with real life. It's like a concert with the tenor changing by the hour.

During the evening the tables slowly fill with Thai people who enjoy salted fish with tender bones, chicken intestines, fat pigskin and all the many delicacies with white rice served on a mix of household utensils like plastic plates and sheet metal dishes. Slow motion keeps on for a while, but after nine o'clock the waitresses start moving. No more time to take long naps with the head on the table.

One of the good things about Laan Sukapok is the absence of background music. Unlike most Thai eateries and bars of that caliber, there is no assault to your ears by either wailing Isaan songstresses or slashing pop music cymbals. Instead there are the sounds of people. Laughing girls, the sputter of Phuket and Isaan dialects, a few noisy farangs and the many languages of Babylon. Pidgin Thai-English is the common nominator. Behind it all flows the accompaniment of traffic. The tuktuks, taxis, Honda Dreams and every ten minutes a young Thai idiot screaming by on one of those high-pitched motorbikes. Then there is an eruption in the kitchen, a giant gush and a cloud of chili that extracts and moves even through the street.

The concert of life crescents after midnight. Bargirls come in for a plate of mee jinn, some of the supermarket and hotel girls in their uniforms, too.

Alas, now the firehouse is gone. It was a special treat at the time we had that Go Go located right next to the Laan Sukapok. The Firehouse ladies would come in for a morsel of Thai noodles and stand at the counter clad in minimalistic French lingerie... Sketchily covered by a sarong, a T shirt or any other piece of garment, so that they would not stand stark naked. But still the exorbitantly high heels, the powerful make-up and the nylons were a sight to see.

The Firehouse girls were a wonderful, soprano counterpoint to the griminess of the surroundings. Sitting with a shandy, catching glimpses of nylons, brassieres and even the adorable small G string undies was pure paradise. Go Go goddesses had come down to earth to sit and suck spaghetti with decollated breasts and all the other outlets of femininity. It was impossible not to think of irregular French verbs.

And then, finally, the golden hour would strike. I don't know how much time I have spent through the years in this eatery, watching the chicks roll in late at night. You see, as all the "downtown" bars close around 2 AM, the girls gyrate towards Soi Sunset, where the action will continue until the break of dawn. In order to get there, they all stride up through Soi Bangla and must pass the intersection of Rath U Thit. That's where the Laan Sukapok sits and when you sit in the Laan Sukapok at this hour, the exodus will pass right by like a grand real life show for free.

For exodus it is. I wonder how many places our universe has, where one can sit and watch hundreds of glorious half naked Asian chicks roll in? All gorgeous, all dressed to kill and all available for a song and a dime?

Sitting in funky old Laan Sukapok between two and three in the morning always made me feel like a Caesar, like Nero, clad in plain clothes, wandering around in the dirty alleys of Rome, exploring the underworld. There is great manpower in beholding so much female beauty, knowing, you can have it all.

Mythological events come to mind, as I watch hundreds of sirens swinging and dancing in their black skirts, golden belts and silvery shoes. Cinderella, Barbarella, Cleopatra. Do you know what I'm trying to say? Nubian princesses with glowing tiaras on their foreheads. Prancing onyx antelopes with high hinds, black unicorns with shining ivory horns.

On and on they come, some of them on motorbikes with their nude thighs and high heels bent at odd angles to meet the pedals.

Many girls cannot stand up against the soul food lures of the Laan Sukapok. They come in and bring with them the late night action fun feeling.

Now they all are wide awake, now they are having a good time. This is where you want to catch them: young and lovely like Girls from Ipanema at the prime time of the night.

Spirits are high. Flower children, kathoeys and Filipino musicians mingle and merge in the concert of life.

Later still the garbage men come to collect the piles of rubbish. That is nothing as prosaic as it sounds. The first thing you notice are the lights. I don't know who has equipped the vehicle, but it always reminds me of that blinking thing in the sky of "Blade Runner". Flashlights on the back and the rear, coloured lights all around the truck. The next thing you notice is the sound of the engine and finally - the stench. The guys cling to the truck like monkeys to a tree. When the truck stops, they jump down and attack the rubbish piles with their bare hands.

I have always admired these guys. Actually I have bestowed my earthly belongings to them. There is wonderful symbolism in giving the last of me to a team of cleaners.

As the hours drift away like sand between a child's fingers, mee jinn gets eaten, Heineken gets drunk and everybody is either merry or pretends to be. Suddenly it is six in the morning and the waitresses do not have to move so much anymore. Finally only a couple of kathoeys and a small group of older bargirls still cling to their tables with the dwindling hope of making a lucky draw.

After a dozen of shandies the dawning world looks grim, spoilt and much too bright. But the waitresses seem more awake than ever and all of a sudden a new breed of visitors pour in.

The decelerating diminuendo of bassoons is quickly being substituted by crisp horns and piccolo flutes as bank clerk and office workers occupy the empty seats. With a quick disapproving glance they take in the kathoey-bargirl scenario and place their energetic bodies in the green and blue plastic chairs. It is wonderful to behold their fresh, polite and clean appearance – especially in a contradictorily trashy place like this. And especially in view of the taken for granted mood of it all. But they don't stay for long. Not more than an hour and they are gone.

From now until noon only a few people are still breakfasting. Usually it is hot already at this time of the day. Thai people are not great breakfasters and most farangs and expats are either still asleep, at the beach or at work already.

Lunch is even slower. Every sensible person rests in the shade, taking a nap. Time for the girls to rinse the vegetables and prepare the meat.

Only from four o'clock in the afternoon things begin to liven up again gradually. The first boozers show up. Hippies with long hair and beards, who have mistaken the direction to Goa, India. Balding beer-bellies, serious drinkers, who don't care about looks any more. And there is always the odd guest or couple with a rucksack or a sports bag. Sometimes - but very seldom - even a spectacled backpacker with his worn copy of "Lonely Planet".

Late evening/early night is soon to come again. And with it a new performance of the endless concert of life.

I have a lot of fond memories of the Laan Sukapok. I awoke early to the sight of a horse munching pineapple in the garden once. My mia noi (second wife) said "mai pen rai". It was just some neighbourly animal paying a visit.

I decided to get up anyway and have myself a drink. The only place to go at that time of day was - you guessed it -

the dirty shop, Laan Sukapok. My old Honda Dream knew the route by heart. All I had to do was to lean back, close my eyes and let it roll.

Laan Sukapok was twinkling its cracked neon lights into the face of dawn, billowing clouds of chili-smoke steamed from its kitchen-corner. In other words, things were what they used to be. I tried to order a bia Chang, but as all the waitresses were busy picking noses and studying the decade-old poster on the wall depicting a fat baby child with oily substance dripping down the surface I had to serve myself. I opened the lid of the coffin - they still had that funky old Thai "refrigerator" filled with ice at that time - and pulled a bottle up from under the ice chunks. I rejected the so-called "bottle opener" - an old, rusty, worn-out thing welded to the metal housing and used a spoon to pry the beer open. Then it started to rain. Right away it was the typical Phuket blow that hits you without any warning. Whosh - there it is, as if somebody pulled the plug on Niagara.

But only few minutes later the heavy rain stopped and turned into a steady fizzle. The world was grey, wet and warm. A tall, blond ladyboy with breasts quelling out of her short sleeved shirt and quivering buttocks stood at the counter in anticipation of a plateful mee jinn... when the monks appeared. First there was one, than there were two and three and four. Like pregnant storks they walked barefoot in the rain, beggar-bowls concealed under the robes.

The ladyboy stiffened. Then she grabbed her freshly arrived food and donated it to the senior monk, who opened his stomach like a creature out of "Total Recall". The noodles disappeared into the womb and the tall, blond lady who once had been a black-haired boy bowed down, fell to her knees and received the monk's blessing.

Rah rah, ohn ohn... Rain, sex, old rite. There was something in the air that morning. Like a wind blowing out of eternity it grabbed my stony heart and made my eyes water. Here I sat on my old plastic chair at the good old Laan Sukapok in the middle of rainy season. And somehow the whole picture - the Nubian princesses, the office clerks, the kathoeys and the pregnant monks all added up to... I do not know what.

Tears in heaven?

Stirrings in the river of time?

The eternally evolving wheel of karma?

Or just fleeing melodies in the fugacious concert of life...?

2. PHUKET DIARY

The Phuket Diary is not Harry's intimate personal diary - but close to. Originally it was written as a blog when he was still living on the island. Here you have it on print in a slightly revamped version.

Low Season Blues

When the dark, misty clouds gather over Mount Kathu and the street vendors cover their banana cakes with plastic film... when the sparkling *zinghs* of rubber tree fruits exploding in the midday heat no longer punctuate the solitudal sound of silence on my hillside veranda... when the waterfalls of Phuket grow big, strong and splashy like the foreign soldiers who invade this island from time to time...

That's when I do some reading the old school way. I actually go to a book store (as long as they exist) or pick a book by the internet - or even blow the dust of some worn old copies I have at home, mostly scientific or philosophic items, and settle in my manila hammock for some good hours of filling intellectual holes in my head.

Writing too, is a gratifying pastime, as my brain slurps wisdom, my soul absorbs relaxation and my fingers play on the keyboard.

Sometimes in the afternoon I let a tuktuk carry my absorbed mind and soul to the herbal spa on Nanai. For an hour and a half my consciousness drifts towards Zen, while experienced hands pamper my body with oil and ambrosias.

Once in a while friends from abroad will come by and stay for a few days and I always enjoy the lengthy conversation with a guest or two at my house. Living in the off-seasons is so laidback.

While my housekeeper or one of the girls who have not left for Isaan on their vacation prepares tom yam gung (shrimp soup), we may discuss matters of the world.

Why does God allow pain and evil in his creation? (So that we have lyrics for Country & Western songs).

Is there life in the universe? (Yes. But Phuket is the navel of the cosmos).

Where do you buy the best ice for your drinks? (At Ning's shop, down at the corner).

And in such manner one off-season day takes the other, while the world spins happily in her odd angle manger.

In other words, I do quite the same things as you do, and as every other farang on Phuket in the wet, wonderful, waterworld offseason does.

But sometimes I feel like doing something different. A sleazy feeling of abenteuerlust creeps into my absorbed body parts and intellectual holes. I feel like... well, having to hit the road even at the risk of a little rain.

What I do is, I go out and re-discover Phuket. Just like in the days of my first visit to this "Pearl of the South". Sometimes I take one of the big bikes, the Harley or the Suzi. But most of the time my little Honda Dream will do. She is easy to maneuver, she shields from the moisture underneath and she carries luggage like the dream she is.

I go where my intuition and my little Honda take me. First gear... it's all right... Just like in the exciting period of the past, where everything was new and wonder. Except that now I know a great deal more. And that is good. I understand, what people are saying - to me and to each other. I know, what the prices are, where to get what and where to look for thrills and adventures that plain tourists will not be able to find.

So. Forget low season blues. Go with me and discover Phuket! Let's see, where the little Honda and 30 Baht worth of gasoline get us. Hop on the bike, Mike.

Country & Eastern

"How much?" the pump attendant asks.

The tank of my little bike holds about 3 liters of petrol. When full. That's 30 Baht, less than two dollars. Less than a bottle of beer.

Well then, let's have a party and fill'er up! That will give me about 100 kilometres on the road, enough for one day's leisurely travel.

Or maybe not? Who knows what a difference a day makes... 24 little hours from now, where will I be?

It feels great to be on the road again. When the low season blues wash over the island with their heavy bellies all black and blue and when the laundry comes back all damp and smelly... when the breakers off the Kata and Patong beaches show their teeth and eat tourists alive... when the monks hide in their temples and huts instead of wandering the misty morning sois... that's when I grab my bike and rediscover Phuket.

It does rain during monsoon season. But still it is just like a hot, if wet, summer. All right, when it rains it rains cats and dogs. But there are those clear days. Like today. By tonight my nose and arms will be burning red. But that's okay.

Further on down the road there is an open air market. A lot of pick-ups and vans. Fifty or more small motorbikes parked at wayside. Many of them are samlors (three-wheelers) with a home-made side car attached to the frame. I stop and find a vacant spot between a rusty old samlor whose third wheel stands at an odd angle to the other two and who's gas tank has been replaced by an old plastic oilcan... and a shiny new street-racer with flashing colours and the misspelled name *new road an-*

gell sprayed proudly on the side. The place is bustling. The first stalls right next to the road sell snacks. Spring rolls, hot cookies and sugar cane juice are being made and sold fresh on the spot. Further on fruit vendors have stacked their wares up high. Mountains of chili paste in red, yellow and brown towering everywhere. Fish, shells, crabs, shrimps... and a fiest for tropic fruit lovers: mango, mangosteen, rambutan, lichee, lamyai, lime and the king of fruits, the mighty and smelly durian. The vegetables on the other hand seem quite familiar to Western eyes: carrots, cabbage, corn, onions and mushrooms abound.

The middle section of the market space belonged to the meat-vendors. Freshly slaughtered chicken, raised in the yard on leftovers from "real food" laid on wooden planks side by side with pigs' ears, noses and intestines.

From the clothes-vendors' stalls comes the monotonous rattle of voices appraising colourful T-shirts copies and cheap bras made in Thailand.

Right in the middle of the market a truck has dumped some P.A. equipment which seems to originate from Chuck Berry's first garage back in the woods 1952. An old synthesizer that must have belonged to Ray Charles in his teens and an antediluvian copy of a Fender bass made in Hong Kong. A microphone like the one from my old tape-recorder four decades ago... But this wondrous collection of museum pieces is not on display or for sale, neither is it a heap of rubbish, I discover. This is the actual road-gear of an authentic upcountry Thai band. While I stand and inspect the musical tools, the musicians enter the "stage". They all have a somewhat funny kind of unsteady walk. The keyboard player feels his way to the stool, which actually is a wooden crate, with his fingers rather than with his eyes. And the singer grabs her microphone while meditatingly looking in a different direction. I do not realise it at first, but when the bass-man is being escorted up to his Hong Kong Fender and has his helper crank up the volume on the amplifier for him, it dawns upon me that this is an all-blind bunch.

Without further ado the songstress intonates a wail that makes my hair stand erect.

"Oioioi..." she goes "ahahaha...."

And one, two, three - voila, the band joins in to the crash of a cymbal. And guess what! They sound incredibly good! The girl's piercing, lamenting voice crisp and clear on top of the instruments full-bodied backdrop.

Fascinated I sit down on an empty wooden fish-crate and open my beer.

A blessing for the musicians, that they cannot see their audience. Nobody really listens, people walk by and carelessly drop a coin or two into the battered old cookie jar in front of the singer's inwardly looking eyes. Actually I, the only white-skinned person in this place, am a greater spectacle for folks to behold. People actually stride up, pretend to listen to the music, but stare at me, their curiosity barely masked by the casual cling of money in the dented old cookie jar in front of the girl with the inward eyes.

The music is strictly Isaan - the Country and Eastern of Thailand so to speak. Lengthy ballads about the love between poor farmers who cannot unite, because parents give their daughters to wealthy landowners as maids and playtoys. About girls, that must go to the big city and sell their love for money.

All songs are in the same key, all melodies are in minor, all the singer's vocals are interspersed with needle-sharp, pentatonic guitar fills. But the mood is not sad. Rather hypnotic and relaxed. Once in a while the guitar-player grabs a bamboo flute, somewhat like a pan-flute, but with the pipes organized in two parallel rows rather than in a semicircle and blows away. The arrangement of the pipes allows him to produce chords as well as melodic fills. Strangely, he makes the flute sound very much like his electric guitar.

The sun is shining, big umbrellas cast shadows over sapodillas, rose-apples, and plastic wares. The air is filled with scents and smells. Of spicy pastes enriched with coconut milk. Of dried fish and smoked squids. Open fires from stalls and samlor-shops that prepare deep-fried pawpias (spring rolls), dried squid and chicken legs with sticky rice give away billowing clouds of smoke.

Smiling, slender girls from Pakarang and Kathu in T-shirts and designer-shorts mingle with big, bargaining mama-sans in ankle-length sarongs. Shy boys and girls from country villages with big eyes cannot help but stare at me, flash their teeth and avert their face, when their eyes meet mine.

Everything breathes peace and leisure. Time flies by while the narratives of love and sorrow spin their haunting web of notes through the scented air. The bottle of beer is empty and my butt hurts from the uncomfortable seat. Menacingly a giant black cloud moves its heavy belly downward from the Kathu mountains with a promise of rain. But the sun prevails and the blinding light creates a spectacular show against the enigmatic backdrop.

Time to move on. I find a 50 Baht note in my pocket and slip it gently into the old tin can. It will be the only one of its kind between all the coins. With the wails of the blind songstress still in my ears and the wind in my hair I ride on. The long and winding road leads through pineapple and rubber tree plantations. Newly pressed rubber mats hang here, there and everywhere. On fencing wires, garden fences, clothes-lines.

A samlor or two drag themselves along coughingly, loaded to the brim with heavy rubber mats. Papa, mum and kids waving happily as I pass them by.

I know there is a waterfall in this area of northern Phuket. This is a good time to visit it and I might as well drop by. No tourists around and lots of water in the fall.

I remember the last time I was on a waterfall trip, ages ago. The woods were gently whispering, the water happily gurgling and the birds caroling... a setting out of wonderland. And the girl... ah. Pink and white flowers tucked in dark, long hair. Pearly white teeth behind ruby red lips.

Well, this time I will tuck a flower in my own hair and let the cascades whisper sweet off-season promises in my ears.

The Joy of Suffering (Vegetarian Delights)

It sounds so innocent and so pure: Vegetarian Festival. Something with carrots and cauliflowers. Something with health and proper diet. You bet not. Well yes - in a way. Hundreds of serene Asian faces, devouring mountains of grey-green Chinese cabbage heads and slurping yucky cabbage soup. 99 monks in carrot-coloured robes walking solemnly around the temples... But beware, such is only the beginning.

Actually, I had seen pictures. Terrifying sights of men clad in square aprons. Walking in street processions with huge monster objects and artefacts like spears, metal rods and saw-blades drilled straight through their gums and cheeks.

But those were just pictures. A picture can never substitute the real experience, no matter how seizing.

You look at it and you say: o*h well...* Nothing forces you to confront reality. And nothing in the pictures had prepared me for the real thing.

So there I was, at five o'clock in the morning, the sandman still in my eyes, standing in the yard of the Jui Tui temple. Bells were ringing, drums were being beaten and people milled around everywhere. The place was bristling with anticipation - and reeking of cabbage soup.

A group of chosen ones lingered in front of the left wing of the alter. *Morituri te salutant.* The death-defying heroes were getting ready to get down with destiny. But they didn't look anything like Caesar's rugged bunch of lion-eaters. Actually they looked a little bit lost, even frightened, as they stood there, facing the task at hand. Doubtful thoughts knocked at the doors of their perception.

ANOTHER NIGHT IN PARADISE

Would it work one more time? Had they cleansed their bodies and souls thoroughly enough? Had they imbibed sufficient heaps of cabbage and other vegetables?

But things were moving up. Heavy fumes from wood and incense filled the temple air, superseding the cabbage reek. The "band" really got into the groove and pushed, pushed, pushed for ecstasy. Already the first men began to show signs of possession. Sweat started to pour, dripping from faces. Eyes became glassy. Movements became obsessed.

Spirits and obsessions are strangely well-known yet largely unknown old friends to humanity. They say dogs are man's best friends. Thus spirits must be man's oldest acquaintances.

I remember my childhood, when everybody towered over me shouting, moaning and speaking in tongues. I remember Billy Graham. Quite the opposite of your sweating, dancing Asian animist. A businessman. In a grey suit and with gold-rimmed glasses before mild, fatherly eyes. Looking benignly at the crowd like a Mafioso boss.

But in his focused mind the intention and the power to create chaos were waiting to be released and shot into the audience like tomahawk missiles with nuclear warheads.

Dear Lord, thank you for blessing this congregation and sending your holy spirit to uplift our burdened souls. Thank you for sharing your divine power!

Good old Graham didn't need a band. He didn't need the ringing of bells. He didn't need clouds of smoke nor firecrackers nor naked, sweaty torsos. He just opened his mouth and hell broke loose. The lame would walk. Crutches zipped through the air. Everybody kept their heads down. The deaf would talk. "Yak, yak, yak" everybody held their hands to the ears. The sick would be healed. The demented started to laugh. It was bedlam.

So why would I stand shivering at the sight of my Phuket friends shoving iron through their faces? It's the pain and torture thing, I guess. Blood, pain and slashing of human tissue is all well in the cinema or on video. But when somebody slowly and deliberately shoves a ten feet rod or chain through his face - right under my nose - it's different. Of course the question you ask yourself, is: does it hurt? It seems like a rather dumb question, doesn't it?

Well... not necessarily. I remember my boxing days when I was young. I would come home with a bleeding nose and swollen lips. And my mother would ask me, didn't it hurt?

Well... it didn't. I never felt any pain. Only the suspense and joy of the fight. When the game was over, I looked in the mirror, saw my bruised face and felt like a hero. In contrast, I was terrified by a nurse's first syringe.

Friedrich Nietzsche thought that the greater the pain, the greater the joy of overcoming it. Sigmund Freud found that the physical and mental make-up of man did not sustain prolonged joy. Only prolonged pain and misery.

Obviously neither Friedrich nor Sigmund have ever been to Thailand. Their tough, Teutonic minds so full of Weltschmerz and joy through despair has never encountered the Thai principle of "sanuk". *Joy through happiness.*

Thai society is ruled by sanuk. You thought it was ruled by the government. But it is not. Sanuk is the sole helmsman in every Thai person's life. I've had a little business once. It came as no surprise that my staff would stop working every time the noodle-vendor drove up on her battered old Honda. And the fried-rice vendor. And the cookie man. I was not surprised when I found them taking a nap with their foreheads on the counter. But it did catch me by surprise the first time one of my staff disappeared and never came back.

"Where is Miss Lek?" I asked my manager.

"Miss Lek who?" she asked back.

I said: "You know, the little person who always wears pink ribbons in her hair."

"Ah, you mean Miss Lek!" the manager exclaimed "She doesn't work her any more!"

"Oh!" I managed to say and looked sheepish.

But why, for God's sake?

"Bog mai mee sanuk."

So she left, because she didn't have enough sanuk! Got me there, buster! I mean - how much can you really expect from life? Here is this little Thai girl. She is raised on rice and water in this poor family back home in Isaan. She borrows money for the bus ticket to Phuket. She gets a job with a farang (me) who pays her double the salary she would get in a similar job anywhere else. So now she can send money back home. The family prospers. Papa can buy a tractor for the rice field. She has a room - which she does not have to share with anybody. She is equipped with a beautiful uniform. She has free meals and gets to feast on noodles, rice, cookies and pancakes by the hour, whenever the noodles-, rice-, cookies- and pancake people drive up on their battered old Hondas. She takes a day off whenever her uncle, sister or brother's, sister's, nephew's stepdaughter has the flu. All day long day I see her laughing and having fun with the other guys on the job. I never recall anybody bossing her around. If she did her job well, she was looking at a promotion and a raise...

And she would **leave** this job? Just like that? One day she goes home after work, without a word, never to return.

"See you tomorrow, Harree" is all she says, lying. Knowing I would **never** see her again... Because the job was not entertaining enough! Miss Lek didn't mind losing thousands of future Baht and dozens of future tractors for her dad's rice-field. As long as she had sanuk right this moment.

I since learned that Thai people will never compromise on this point. Sanuk comes first and sanuk comes last! You think I am rambling, don't you? Well here's the issue: why would any Thai person submit to suffering and pain by their own free will? Why would anybody shove several meters of heavy metal through their faces? Why would anybody beat themselves with axes, slice their feet with knives and stick needles through their tongues?

In order to understand a phenomenon like the Vegetarian Festival one must consider the fact that contrasts tend to entwine themselves in a mystery called paradox. How can the very concept of "sanuk" exist in the first place - in a society that is predominantly Buddhist? Buddhism preaches the end of suffering through turning your attention inward and through the resistance against the temptations of the flesh.

In Thailand everybody lives happily with the dualism of the mind and the flesh. Buddha says: *Flee the unreal world of the flesh. Close your senses. Open your mind only to nothingness.*

In your books and travel guides you will read that Thailand is a society where everybody believes - and follows

- the teachings of Buddha. But this is not so. Basically, Thai people are animists just like the majority of their brethren and sisters throughout South Asia. Nothing has changed, really, since Buddha held his divine speeches.

Forget animism, Buddha said. Do not believe in all those phees, spirits and bloodsucking monsters that live in trees. Use your good mind. Think reason! Act naturally! Make the right choices! And your lives will improve. And he added: *I am not a god. I will go into nirvana, because I desire no more. But please, don't make a god out of me after I'm gone! Don't erect any statues of me!*

The people listened to the wise words of Buddha. They understood his picture of the world. They took his preaching to their hearts. So much, that they not only incorporated him in the long row of heavenly and earthly spirits, but even made him the boss of the spirits. They made him God. Now they pray to him just like they pray to the very same spirits, he so hard tried to dethrone. So now you have spirit-houses with phees and Wats with Buddhas standing side by side. Just as you have sanuk and abstinence side by side.

A wonderful symbol of the paradoxical co-existence of sensuality and forsakenness are the beer advertisements at the Vegetarian Festival. Here you have all these people that have to refrain from sex and sin and alcohol. They have cleansed their minds and souls for nine long weeks. They wear white robes. And they carry those bloody beer-ads on their shirts! If Buddhism is the mental depletion of the senses, animism is their carnal fulfilment.

So, dear Friedrich and Sigmund: Forget the troublesome path to enlightenment through sublimation of pain and neuroses. Here you have transcendency through sweet, passive, indulgent nothingness. Or even through the opposite: luscious, sybaritic pleasure-seeking.

I asked a friend of mine, who had joined the ranks of vegetarian heroes once, and done the un-do-able. He had speared himself through the face and he had walked on burning charcoal. Being farang!

So back to the question in question. Had he felt pain?

No.

Had he felt anything else?

Yes.

Like what?

Well... mostly hot. Not really sweaty, but kind of hot from the inside of the brain.

It is a common experience that important pivot points in people's lives are emotional blanks or have some kind of retarded fuse to them.

A good many situations that have changed a set of patterns in my life or have abrupted major strings of events still give me the shivers today - many years later. But I do not recall any strong emotions while the crucial events actually were in progress.

I remember when I was eight years young. I had this piano-teacher who was an absolute sadist. I used to hate Sundays, when coming from Sunday-school, I picked up my Bach or Beethoven at home and boarded the subway-train. At my teacher's house I would begin to feel cold. Entering the hallway with its all too familiar smells and the flowerpot in the corner made we want to throw up. Ringing the bell and being let into the flat of my torturer was like entering Hades. I won't go into details according to what happened in there. The point I want to make is this: after months of abuse by the old goat I finally and suddenly had enough. I found myself leaving the piano-bench, quietly gathering my Bach and Beethoven sheets and putting them into my bag. I didn't feel anything. Or rather, I had a remote awareness. I saw the whole situation from the outside. The real me was hovering in space, looking at a miniaturized double, picking up his stuff and bravely exiting the scene.

Seeing, hearing and smelling the not so bloody miracles of the Vegetarian Festival for the first time pushed my frontiers of prejudices a quantum leap ahead. Suddenly it was not a mere picture any longer. Suddenly I realized that this had nothing to do with drugs or faking things or devil worshipping.

I could relate a tiny little bit through the perception of myself, picking up my Beethoven and doing the undoable, while my mind rested empty in space. What had I felt, back then? Not much. Maybe a little cold? Warmth? Shiver?

Among the hundreds of images that I saw and witnessed that morning at Wat Jui Tui is one that I will never forget. On the right side in front of the alter a group of women had gathered to prepare themselves for the penetrating of their flesh. One of the women was a slim, pretty and rather little lady. She stood with closed eyes in front of the statues of the Nine Emperor Gods, preparing to let one of them enter her mind and possess her body. Two female helpers arranged the elaborate ruffles on her pink, magenta and white dress, while she was meditating.

When the power of the gods gripped her, she danced out into the yard to have her cheeks penetrated. I wondered which of the provided instruments of horror would be the object of her choice. The bamboo spear with the feathers attached? The transparent water hose with living guppies in it? Or the spikes from a bicycle wheel? The entranced lady pointed at the golf club. I do not know, what she felt, when they rammed the club through her face. I do not know whether she played golf herself. But she sure looked wonderful, as she rose up from the chair and strode up to join the other processionists. The steel club reflected blazing sunrays from between her jaws. A little drop of blood had trickled down her chin and made a red dot on the white blouse, that was all. It looked like a tiny rose.

I don't know if she felt a little bit like the eight year old kid, doing the un-doable in the presence of his torturer. But I know what I felt, when I saw her: I felt the beauty of the whole, bloody thing. It was all coming together. The sun, the sanuk, the spirits. Bach, Beethoven and Sigmund. Vegetables, spirits and burning coal.

It was a leap of faith and a magic moment of understanding nothingness and feeling fulfilment.

3. TURNING THE TABLES

Watching the Water fall

Finally I did it. I let myself be caught, handcuffed and prisoned in the holy jail of marriage. Her name was Nang and she had a graceful motion that made her stand out, even though she wasn't nearly as beautiful as some of the other girls and stunners I had been with. But in her case, beauty did not count as much as - well, personality and grace. She was The One. So I switched from alcoholic to monogamic. I hasten to say that our marriage was a Buddhist Thai wedding, so it was not legally binding. I still had a backdoor open :-)

We were sitting on the big bed together with a couple of friends, munching shrimp-flavoured rice-cookies and shoe-leather, camouflaged as dried squid. Watching one of the countless TV shows on one of the countless channels.

As the picture showed a map of Trang - a southern district, famous for its many waterfalls - Nang, my beloved, said: "Let's visit my sister!"

I asked: "Where does your sister live?"

"Not far from here" she replied "just south of Phuket, close to this huge, wonderful waterfall. You will loove it, teerak. And remember, we have to bring our bathing suits!"

She went on: "Let's rent a car. A black one! I'll pay."

And so we did and so she did. The next day we rented a four wheel driven Japanese kind of jeep copy thing. Which was ridiculous, as the ride from Phuket to Takua Pa consists of some 200 kilometres mirror-smooth asphalt highways, made for red Italian sport cars, not for black rugged four wheeled, deep profiled mountain runners. Except, that is ... for the last three kilometres up to Nang's sister's. After a smooth journey through green and verdant forests lining the grey-blue mirror-asphalt, Nang suddenly exclaimed: "Slowly teerak. This is it. Turn right onto that road by the supermarket."

But it wasn't a supermarket and it wasn't a road. The supermarket was a wooden construction with dried leaves for a roof, a few bundles of bananas dangling from a wooden pillar and a shady concrete seating arrangement in front for the lao khao drinkers. And the road wasn't a road but a dry riverbed. Steep as the path to the Pearly Port, filled with holes as deep as bathtubs and clogged with huge, bumpy, sharp stones. I suddenly wished we had rented a real jeep or even a tank instead of this Japanese tin can copy.

There were no human settlements around. Just rainforest interspersed with parcels of rubber trees and lumps of other utility plants such as coconut, banana and papaya. Occasionally an old Honda bike would be parked at wayside, its owner busy collecting bananas or just picking his nose. Whenever this person got us in his sight, he or she would stop and stare, eyes popping. One hand paralyzed somewhere in its motion between the knees and the nose.

While the kids would wave and holler halloh! Or, farang! Or even halloh farang!

Finally Nang told me to pull over and park the tin can. This was it. The middle of nowhere. We had arrived at our destination.

So where was the dwelling of Nang's sister? If there was a home here, let alone a house, I definitely couldn't see it. But Nang hastened happily up a slope and into the jungle.

Along an overgrown path we went. Tropical trees, roots, lianas and occasionally a shining little orchid flower strutting over our heads. Butterflies. Lots of butterflies. Small black ants, big red ants, small lizards, big lizards, beetles, spiders, snakes, okapis, crocodiles, elephants, whale sharks, vampire bats... At one point I paused and looked around me. And I swear I saw a werewolf's ugly face protrude from behind a poisonous bush.

"Do you have spirits, yetis or other monsters around here?" I asked Nang's behind.

She had taken her high-heels off and trotted along on naked feet, shoes dangling on one hand, balancing herself on tree trunks and stones with the other.

She turned and said matter of fact: "Sure. Of course."

"Do you believe that, too?"

Nang paused hesitatingly.

"Well, yes! Every part of the land has its phees (spirits)."

Her eyes grew concerned as she glanced at the rhinos, giraffes and mammoth's hovering behind me, breathing down my collar. "Okay, let's go quickly! We're almost there!"

And behold! Suddenly I heard the sound of civilisation. From a pile of bamboo sticks and banana leaves came loud and clear the two-voiced fanfare of TV's Channel Seven.

"Eh..!" shouted Nang. "Kai jooh mai (anybody home)?"

Yes, they were home. Gathered in the pile of bamboo sticks and banana leaves - which by closer look turned out to be quite a big and comfortable house - in front of the TV set. Where else? A warm welcome and lots of polite wais' to the longnosed stranger (me). Nang grabbed the bag (which I had been carrying) and out came the neatly laced up truss of rock lobsters that we had purchased at a road stall along the way. Whenever Thai people meet, getting down to eat is the first order on the agenda. And getting down to eat it was, as the house had virtually no furniture except two big beds. This was not a sign of poverty, of course. Just Thai country style.

So we sat down - not on a bed, but on a mat in front of the house. Nang, Noi, her sister, Lek, the sister's husband, Somrak and Deng, Noi and Lek's kids, Oy, a neighbour, who happened to be on a visit, Ning, the neighbours daughter and the white longnose (me).

Somebody produced a fan for the sweating longnose (me) and somebody else found a car-battery to plug it onto. It was the slowest moving fan I had ever seen. But it did help some.

The crabs got cooked right there between the eight of us. As the pot boiled up steam, one of the women took a couple of crabs at a time and threw them into the pot, rushing the lid upon the luckless creatures. One of the animals tried to escape the burning nirvana by leaping out of the pot and into my lap. To stricken by the turn of events I just sat frozen while the crab leaped on, sideways, fast as lightning. With hooting and laughter the thing was recaptured and shoved into the broth one more time.

There is nothing like a good meal of crabs in the jungles of Nakua Pa. The whispering palms and the silent flutter of butterflies mingle with the occasional shlomp of a falling coconut, the zinng of an exploding rubber tree nut and the wails and shrieks of the audience on the TV show, hooked on another battery. The yetis and werewolves had pulled themselves back in favour of friendlier animals like Phoo the housecat with a mouse between her fangs. Even a flying squirrel could be seen shortly, performing a wonderful sail from tree to tree.

Time passed, while a bundle of very arroi (tasty) living crabs got converted into a basketful of shells and spidery legs.

"Let's go to the waterfall!" said Nang.

"But first we must sleep" answered Noi.

Which of course - as everybody knows - is item number two after the meal (preferably crabs) on the agenda whenever Thai's meet.

So everybody fell asleep as on commando more or less at the spot. I chose the shady elevated platform made out of wood and bamboo under a cluster of coconut trees. Nobody laid down on the giant beds. I guess it was just too hot inside.

One of the kids came and joined me, careful at first, so as not to be eaten by a white and gruesome longnose. But curiosity prevailed and finally the toddler sat down close to my head, watching this strange creature (me) and its strange light and wavy hair. I was laying on my back, lazily gazing at the blue sky behind the plait of green leaves. My mind drifting.

As everybody knows after a good sleep the social agenda of the Thai people demands a little snack to replace the lost calories while snoring away. So while everybody got busy absorbing food again (baked bananas and sticky rice this time) I just turned and slept on. When - if ever - would we go and see the fabled waterfall?

I awoke to cheerful chatter and other happy noises, as three brown kids (two of them naked), three women with almond eyes and high cheekbones (in faded sarongs) and Lek the soldier (in Lacoste shirt and designer shorts) were sitting on the ground around another snack of grey and green shoe-leather, disguised as dried squid. The sun was painting impressionistic patterns of moving paper fantasies over the scenery from a low angle. Strutting chicken picked at scraps and heaps with abrupt motions, while Pooh the cat chased a dragon fly across the yard.

I stretched and yawned, feeling at peace with the world deep down inside. Nang caught me with her eyes and beckoned me to come and join the picnic. Slowly, I erected my long-nosed corpus and sat one foot tentatively on the soil.

There is nothing more peaceful on earth than an outdoor nap under a cluster of palm trees in Nakua Pa. I left the elevated platform and sat down beside my wife, who jostled a piece of shoe-leather in between my lips. Which I sat chewing reluctantly but faithfully (the leather, not the lips).

I still sat chewing on the same piece an hour later when everybody had finished their meal and Lek the soldier opened a bottle of lao khao, euphemistically called "Thai Whisky".

"Au mai (like some)?" he asked and produced a glass that easily could hold 50% of the bottle's contents.

"Not really, thank you very much!" I replied politely but firmly.

Lek nodded approvingly, poured approximately half a liter into the giant glass and handed it to me with a big smile and nod. What could I do but accept? Nang saw it and gave me a dirty look. I lifted my shoulders in despair and waited for an unobservant moment to dump the poison on the ground. But Lek watched me intently and smiled with his tooth gap showing.

"You want ice...?" the soldier asked, taking the lid of a thermo-box.

Gosh, they had ice in this place! I cried: "Oh yes, please! The more the better!"

Lek looked at me with undisguised admiration and put the lid back on without handing me any. Empty. Out of ice. He fished out the ice cubes in his own drink with two fingers and threw them away. Lifted his glass and said: "Bottoms up!"

Or something to that respect. Thai people love to party. Sanuk - fun - is the most important thing in Thailand. And that is probably the thing that most definitely sets Thai and farang cultures apart. Doesn't every longnose carry a load of duty and plights on his shoulders as well as a heavy rock of responsibility under his heart..?

The Leks' and Nois' and Nangs' of this land could teach the rest of us a lesson or two... if we were only able to learn.

Which we are not. Because we are predestined to follow the early influences and brainwashes that make us react according to the programs in our blood.

Even when happy, I sit and contemplate; I experience my happy state as something set apart from the "me" that is me.

While my Thai friends and their happiness are one and the same, I and my happiness are two and different. They simply are happy. I sometimes have a happy time. My happiness is a precious guest who flees as soon as other thoughts or worries cross my mind.

Actually I, being a Westerner, am the one that needs to drown my unhappiness in a bottle, as we say. And suddenly it hits me that this saying is false. You do not drown anything in an empty bottle, do you? The more you drink, the less you drown... actively speaking.

Thais do something quite different: They fish happiness out of almost anything, anywhere. Even out of a lao khao bottle. Just like ice-cubes.

Speaking of which... It makes a big difference, which bottle you fish from. A bottle of vodka might give you a slight shake the next day. A glass of good vine may make you lazy. German beer may upset your stomach. But Thai whisky... let me tell you brother!

But to be honest, until hangover begins there is nothing in the world like a bottle of serious rice-booze on a sunny tropical afternoon in the rainforest of Phang Nga. The flying squirrels dance with werewolves in the shade of the old coconut trees. Pooh the cat ties yellow ribbons around the old wishing well. And the frogs... ah, the frogs!

Thailand has the world's biggest variety of frogs, I am sure. They come in all seizes, shades, colours and walks of life. Thai frogs live in seas, puddles, drainage pipes, and wet underwood. They survive on rooftops, in the radiator of Japanese cars and in the swimming pools of the big hotels.

They even thrive on my toothbrush and behind my bathroom mirror. I had a frog that crawled into the drainage pipe of my bathroom every evening at sundown. This animal - who's physiognomy has a worrying likeliness with Lek the soldier's face whenever I drink lao khao without ice in Phang Nga's verdant green forests - then sat for hours quaking and squawking into the hollow pipe that amplified his voice like a bassoon. Every night Little Dipper became Big Bass Boomer. And as the potency and the rank of a male frog and his popularity with the female auditorium is judged by the power of his voice, not by the frame of his body or the size of his organ, Little Dipper was the King of the Swamp behind my house...

And while the frogs and the cicadas of Phang Nga initiated their daily night concert, my mind drifted...

At one time I came to and realized that Nang was helping me out of my clothes.

"Do you know that the rank, potency and reputation of the male frog are determined by the power of his voice?" I asked her.

"Shooh teerak" Nang whispered "don't wake up the house! You're no frog."

The next morning was wonderful... A blessed silence, punctuated only by sweet, longing calls of the golden-throated honey bee, accompanied by the murmur of brook-water running towards the sea.

While a deep-orange fireball of sun rose slowly from behind the waterfall, a million tiny drops of crystal clear water sprinkled titillating rainbows in multilevel curtains through the morning mist. Moist emanation from bamboo thickets, giant spearhead-grasses and vine-trees with leaves smooth as plastic merged with the sprays from the waterfall into a woven kilt, much like the backdrop to Indiana Jones (in colours) or the musty film on an old Tarzan movie (in black and white)...

Or so I was told. In the place where I awoke, things were a little bit different. Bright rays of sunshine were piercing through my closed eye-lids like awls. Images of squawking frogs with wings like leaping squirrels holding toothbrushes in drainage pipes danced on my retina.

The fan had stopped turning, the battery was empty. It was hot and humid. Inside my head thousand vampire-bats were biting and chewing away at the tissue that once had been my brain. Somebody had attached a flaming iron ring to my forehead.

Thus are the punishments for drinking Thai firewater! Especially the one called lao khao.

I remember a painting on the wall of Wat Phra Nang Sahn, a temple in Talang, Phuket, that depicts the torments of the doomed souls in hell. One section of the twenty foot high picture portrays red and horned devils forcing hot burning fluid from a big boiling witches brew kettle into the mouths of the sinners. Nothing could more vividly describe what I was feeling right now.

Brushing through the curtain, Nang's face appeared.

"Uih, so you're finally awake! Go get a shower! Here's a towel."

On the way to the bathroom I passed though the kitchen. Noi and the two kids, Nang, and Lek the soldier were seated on the floor around a big bowl of rice and an even bigger bowl of hot soup. Lek pointed to the food with a spoon. Have some lunch! He looked suspiciously fresh, sporting his designer shorts and a soldier's cap.

The bathing water in the big, green plastic tub had a pleasant temperature. Refreshing, but not cold. Mild, but not hot. As I splashed the soothing liquid over my body, I wondered whether today I would see the fabled waterfall further on up the road. A little frog leaped out of my way as I reached for the towel that I had put on a nail in the woodwork.

I heard cheerful sounds from outside. Oi the neighbour was here again and so was another visitor. With another two kids. The news had spread. Farang in da house!

"Farang, farang! Come and look!"

Yes the word had spread. By the time of the next meal I expected the house would be packed.

A knock on the door. Nang. Was I decent yet? Her sister needed to do some shopping at the market. So could they please borrow the car?

Well... who was going to do the driving?

Why, the sister of course!

Did she have a driver's license?

"A what?"

Had she ever driven a car before?

Well, no. But she was used to motorbikes. And the market was just a few meters down the main road anyway!

"Okay honey" I said "I'll take you there myself."

We squeezed ourselves into the car. Nang, Oy, the two neighbours, me, and the kids. All five of them. All ten of us. Don't ask me how we fitted into the little Japanese tin can!

We arrived at the market in grand style, dust and gravel spluttering off our wheels. The ladies and their offspring climbed out and milled all over the place, fondling the meat and the vegetables, marvelling at the household goods and testing the faded sarongs from Chiang Mai, the screamingly coloured T-shirts and shiny plastic shoes from Bangkok.

I bought a coke with lime and ice from a smiling old lady with only one tooth and a face like a wrinkled rambutan and sat down on a bench in the shade of a mango tree. The weather was hot and humid and very still. But not for long.

Eventually I kind of dozed off a little bit. By the time Nang and Co. came back from their shopping spree dragging giga packs of shopping goods (how on earth were we going to stow all that paraphernalia?), black clouds had emerged and gusty winds coughed over the market-place. The vendors reached for plastic sheets to cover their displays.

"Get in the car, leo leo (quickly)!"

By the time we got back to the riverbed that led to the little house in the jungle, I once again wished we had rented a real mother jeep instead of a Japanese tin can. The rainstorm was only minutes old but already streaming water and cascading pebbles made the "road" an ordeal.

I parked the car in the middle of the river and we all ran towards the house with sixteen tons of shopping luggage and a bottle of lao khao. Raindrops were not only falling on our heads... they were exploding all around us like water bombs.

After only a few seconds in the rain everyone was soaked to the bone. Nang was definitely looking like a Miss Wet T-shirt contestant. Her sister and the neighbours in wet sarongs looked, well... wet.

Safely back in the house everybody changed into dry clothes. Lek the soldier was having a nap in one of the huge beds, cap over his eyes.

There is nothing more cosy in the world than sitting in a jungle abode a rainy afternoon in the rainforests of Phang Nga.

The heavy rains performed drumming solos Gene Krupa style on the roof. All the small rivers coming down from leaks and holes in the roof and alongside the woodworks united to form a mini Mekong delta on the kitchen floor, where the kids were playing Loy Kathoi with banana leaves and croaking frogs for flowers. A mighty fire in the stove was heating rice and water for a round of khao tom gai, chicken soup with rice. Noi grabbed an unsus-pecting chicken by the neck and slammed its head on the chopping block. The children cheered.

"Let's have a snack while we're waiting for the food" Nang suggested. And made for deep fried bananas and sour mangos with sugar and chili, recently bought at the market.

Maybe we would never make it to the waterfall. But the waters falling from heaven right now and the roaring waves of freshwater streams pulling at the jeep outside, threatening to float it away, were a waterfall-like experi-ence in themselves. The waterfall had made it to our house...

"Have a cup of tea and await your destiny" a German saying that I learned from Wolfgang goes. And so I did. Sipping tasteless green chai jeen, Chinese tea, sitting propped up against a pillow on one of the big beds, watching a Thai show-master dressed like an old Egyp-tian king leading candidates, cameras and audience through the logistics of the show.

Outside a marvellous live-concert had begun, even more artistic than the nightly competition. High, higher and even shrill tenors twittered disneyesk mini-melodies into the solar eclipsed afternoon. Bassy croaks performed polyphonic punch-lines. No prince in his high castle has ever lived a fuller life than one of these bewitched frogs, strumming away in the dripping wet riverbed jungles of Phang Nga.

"So what would you do, if you suddenly saw the boy you love in the soda pub sitting with the prettiest girl of the school, holding hands?"

"I would punch him on the nose!" the young lady an-swers emphatically and the audience shrieks with laughter while applauding madly. The mild faced Egyptian show-master with Mongolian eyes shakes his head in sorrow.

"So would he be able to do anything to mitigate you?"

"Well, yes" the girl blushes slightly "He could buy me a golden ring."

The audience shrieks again.

"With a big stone in it!"

The audience shrieks even wilder.

This is the way to show your love in Thailand. Give her gold!

Here comes the ten thousand dollar quiz question: Do the poor girls living in the rainy jungles of Phang Nga carry golden rings on their fingers and 24 carat golden laces around their necks?

Yes! Of course they do! They may go to the market dressed in wet, faded sarongs, but they would never consider doing so without their gold!

According to Nang, Lek the soldier was paid 800 Baht a month for his services. That's 32 dollars.

I had seen two golden rings on Noi's fingers and a lace with a big, triangular, golden Buddha around her neck. How could Lek afford things like that?

"Noh!" Nang exclaimed "Lek couldn't give her gold! He is just a poor soldier. These are gifts from the family!" Meaning: from her own her sweet self, as she had been the only one making fundamental sums with farangs in distant Pakarang.

One has to understand that rural Thais are not in the habit of buying insurances. They may not put any money in the bank, either. They just carry their savings around their necks and on their fingers everywhere they go. The more the better.

Which immediately puts a question in the Westerner's mind: don't they get robbed?

The funny thing is, Lek's and Noi's house didn't even have a lock on the door. It would have been futile anyway, as the house had no window panes.

All is not gold, that shines. If you rise early and work hard, you will earn the golden pot at the rainbows end... or something to that respect.

Never seemed any wisdom more obscure than these old worlds.

Thai people like to sleep. Thai people like to eat. Thai people like to party. Thai people want to be happy right now. Not in the next life, not next year. Not even next week. But right here and now, today, this afternoon.

Ah, we have so much to learn from them. Thailand, the "Land of Smiles" is exactly that. A country, whose entire population smiles because that is the natural mood of her citizens and the way it ought to be.

One cannot help but wonder whether Thai people pay a price for their happiness? There is no such thing as a free lunch!

Really? This saying does not apply here.

And what about happiness? As Freud puts it, happiness by nature tends to last only very short. Quickly unhappiness, sadness and hurt take its place. The human body and soul holds so many receptors for pain and so little capacity for joy.

When I sit down on the floor, my back will kill me after five minutes. When I eat, I can only enjoy for so long. But I can linger in hunger and pain for ever. Whatever I do, whichever situation I enjoy - it always turns into pain after a short while. Joy has a short lifespan, but pain never stops.

Well, Thai people have been able to outsmart nature and stretch their moments of happiness into an everlasting waterfall of precious delightful hours and days of constant joy. They do so by always and uncompromisingly grabbing for instant fun instead of long-time reward. This carries punishment in itself for the Western mind. It is the exact reversal of the ethics my parents taught me. By abstaining from short-time pleasure, the reward would be even greater long-time pleasure, they said.

As we all know by now, it doesn't work like that. Thais live to prove. But we stubbornly believe that there is no other way.

"The human body is made for pain" grandmaster Freud said. But old Sigmund never experienced Thailand. If he had lived on Phuket instead of in Vienna, psychoanalysis would never have been born.

Thus we must learn: never put off till tomorrow the sanuk you can have today.

If somebody gave me a choice: Get one dollar today or get a hundred dollar next week! I'd choose the hundred next week. But Thai people live by a different tune. The half-empty glass of water is in reality always half-full. Do you win one dollar today... or do you lose 99 dollars by not waiting until next week?

Answer: The problem does not arise, as the question is not allowed to enter your mind.

It is pretty simple, really. In reality there is no connection between the one dollar gained and the 99 dollars lost. Bob Dylan got it right: How many times can a man turn his head, pretending he just doesn't see.

Except for the world "pretend". There is no pretending here. Just a mind that from the time of birth has been trained to see the upper side of every coin. And two hands that have been trained to grasp for happiness in every situation.

Remarkably, Buddhism is a philosophy that offers its followers no sugarplums. No heaven with eternal delights. No Christian afterlife in the great choir of angels. Not even grand Islamic retaliation at the sight of enemies roasting like chestnuts in an open fire. Buddhism has no god, offers no reward but total annihilation and everlasting nothingness.

You see, I have been living in Thailand quite some time, and though I never will reach Nirvana, and though I not even will reach the Thai happy state of mind ever, I have learned a few things.

For instance, two days ago, Nang and I set out to see a waterfall.

"Let's go" she had said "you will love the waterfall, teerak".

And so we went. But things change along the way. Philosophically speaking, the act itself changes reality by bending the paths of probability. Niels Bohr has said: Looking at something changes it.

And besides - who wants to walk a mile for some water splashing down a cliff, when they can have an Egyptian show-master live on the telly?

Therefore, in a quantum-mechanical sense, I did not really envision reaching and seeing the waterfall as the true goal of our trip. If we would reach the waterfall eventually - all well and good. If not - well, then our trip would have had another climax, another destination. Being able to transcend the Western feeling of result-orientation and being able to replace it with a love for whatever the future holds... this is the biggest lesson, I can hope to learn.

The highest goal that I, a man with a Freudian mind, can strive for.

Que sera, sera, we say. *Laissez faire* is another expression of the same thought. Though very different from the happy *mai pen rai* (it doesn't matter) - laissez faire like que sera is rather an apathetic, fatalistic attitude - it gives us farangs a merely a translated picture of the Thai way of achieving happiness through being gentle and through floating with the stream of un-consciousness instead of battling it.

Stoically, not quantum-philosophically speaking: what is the difference between watching a waterfall fall and watching an Egyptian show-master mastering his job on channel Seven? It is all in the mind, really.

But before we reach a philosophical point of no return, let us go back to the little house in the rainy forests of Phang Nga.

I did not linger in front of the TV set for ever. The second car battery also ran dry after a while and the rain eventually stopped just as dramatically as it had begun. The drumming of Gene Krupa on the roof disrupted itself in one sudden instant. At the same moment the sun broke shining through, spraying golden lacquer on everything in sight. The frogs still croaked like mad and the river outside the house kept flowing for a while. But finally everybody seemed ready for some action.

"The Thai spirit, if released, is a marvel" as our local newspaper has it.

Suddenly everybody was holding bags, blankets, and kids in or under their arms.

"Let's go" Nang said plainly.

"Go where?" I guffawed.

"To the waterfall, melonhead!"

The road was slippery and muddy. Good luck, we had rented a car with a four wheel drive. Driving sideways as much as head-on (and even backwards) we wearisome climbed the slope towards the waterfall. Yet nothing gave away the presence of such a phenomenon so far. All we could see were jungle and rubber trees. No mountains, no rivers, no lakes.

Until suddenly the long and winding road disappeared, giving way to a wide plateau, perfect for a parking space. Nang, her sister Noi, the two kids and I hopped, crawled, sprang out of the car and proceeded along an overgrown path underneath dripping trees, casting shadows in the fierce sunshine. Humid haze rose from the foliage like steam from a hot plate.

It was so beautiful! It was Christmas and Easter Parade and birthday at the same time. At every turn in this Spielberg movie I half expected giant pythons to appear and bare their poisonous smiles or white elephants with Nubian princesses on their back. The combination of dripping wet, atavistic vegetation and laughingly loud sunshine made up a fascinating and compelling scenery.

Finally the path through the undergrowth joined another plateau. Small streams of water gurgled downhill. The trees grew sparse and allowed me to look forward and upward, and...

There it was! Nang's waterfall.

A mighty rock jutted up from the watery plateau like a giant's fist. From between the "knuckles" on top, several cascades of sparkling white water gushed down with a vengeance. The sound the fall made resounded a little bit like an old, rumbling freight-train carrying the Domspatzen choir with pubescent boys shushing the initial notes of a Christmas carol. Or something to that liking. A little indefinable, but very impressing, very sudden and very unexpected.

At the bottom, where we stood, the rock formed several shallow basins with very clear water. The biggest one was double the size of the swimming pool at the Holiday Inn. The smallest one had the size of a baby bathtub.

Incredibly, my Thai friends found a non-wet, almost dry spot of "grass" and spread out a blanket. Within seconds, Nang had stripped off her clothes, revealing a red and black one-piece bathing suit and jumped into the water. Clearly, this spot was well known to her. She dived head-on into the pool from a three meters high protrusion off the cliff, where the incessant pounding of the water had dug out a deep well.

The children quickly followed Nang's example and frolicked in the shallower waters. Noi tightened her sarong, entered the water slowly and sat down on a stone to watch over the kids.

Nang splashed her way back to me through the basins and laughingly helped me undress. I looked around and found Noi standing still beside me, staring. Then she whispered something in Nang's ear.

"What is it" I asked, taken aback.

Noi uttered something and shamefully tried to avert her eyes and close her mouth, but the draw was to strong.

"What did she say?"

Nang smiled: "Your skin is so white."

I looked down at my body and legs. White?

Ah, yes. Noi had never been to the soft-sanded beaches of Phuket, where lily-white farangs lie in heaps, basking in the sun. And I had to admit - as a lone, Caucasian Tarzan amongst four sapodilla-skinned natives in the jungle-waters of Phang Nga I looked kind of odd... well, a little bit freakish, almost. Like Michael Jackson in Africa, maybe. So I made a sexy Michael Jackson pirouette and let my lily white self fall into the water. The water was actually not too cold, but refreshing. And it tasted sweet and pure.

After a lot of splashing and enjoying the tumbling streams we sat down to devour sticky rice and mangoes, relaxing after our efforts. But I felt like exploring some. A trail led straight up the rock on our side of the waterfall. I asked Nang to come along. But she wasn't in the mood for any more strains on one day.

So I took a bottle of water and strode off into the wilderness.

The first part was a fairly steep uphill climb. But nooks and crannies in the rock and the trunks and roots of vegetation gave good foothold. After few minutes my body was wet with perspiration, even though I moved in the shadow of trees and ferns. The humidity had to be as close to a hundred as it ever would.

On top of the hill was a glorious little lake. Only few centimetres deep, enclosed by the finest brown sand that the water had carried downstream. Twigs, leaves and flowers mirrored themselves in the quiet surface. Tiny fish and even crabs hurried to and fro. I sat down and instead of drinking water from my plastic-bottle I savoured the water from the mountain. It was delicious, cool and sweet. The scenery was one of unspoiled nature, complete with the heavy smell of rainforest - that reminded me of the greenhouses of my childhood - and the sounds of animals. Birds cooing and twittering. An occasional flurry of wings among the leaves. Lizards and small rodents hastening through the thicket. Insects buzzing and chirping. A perfect place to sit and meditate for a while. The monks had it right, as well as the artists and the romantics. In the bosom of nature calm and soothing thoughts enter our minds and push our souls closer to the pantheon of cosmos.

Sitting alone and undisturbed in the beauty of God's creation, man's spirit are uplifted, his soul opens to the divine voice. There is no need for disco music or internet chattiness in nature's embrace. Eternal peace and tranquillity prevail.

Until, that is, you have to go to the toilet. Which in spite of the lack of rest room facilities provided no problem. I was completely alone, and there was water everywhere. I mean, nature is full of living creatures, even mammals who share their sustentation by giving back their valuable reminiscences to soils and plants.

At Turning Point

I decided to venture further and left the little lake behind. Following the creek upstream, the overgrown trail led up a gentle slope in ever winding turns.

After about twenty minutes I reached another plateau and another lake. This one was as deep and sinister as the first one had been shallow and friendly. The sun shone glaringly bright on its surface, creating chilling black shadows where the lake disappeared into a big and deep grotto.

I sat down on the rim - the lake was contained by a natural dam - a wall rising steeply up from the slope. At one side at the edge of a water basin a small amount of water leaked out of the bowl, thus creating a miniature waterfall. No telling how deep the water was in the basin. In contrast to the shallow first lake "downstairs" this one was not clear, but looked muddy and hostile. I could not make out the bottom. Not even the fingers of my submerged hand at arm's length.

From where I sat I could not see much ahead either. The wall of naked rock rose threateningly behind the lake like a fortress. On top and on its one side ample vegetation prevailed. The rock itself was hollow. A mighty, black grotto opened in the middle.

I decided to test the waters. Something about this menacing cave challenged me. It beckoned.

"You are a different man now, Mr James" it said. "You have abolished your former life as a prowling Fox amid lovely Thai chickens. You have decided to be true and faithful to your chosen lady."

It didn't make sense, but I knew exactly what the voice was telling me. I had made a decision a few days earlier,

I was going to leave the blissful shores of Pakarang. Something about Nang and her firm acknowledgement of me as a person, as her lover and husband had made a difference.

Maybe you think that Thai girls are all soft and submissive. Chances are you have seen pictures of fat old men together with youngish and sweet looking Thai girls so often, you actually believe in the old stereotype. But let me tell you, most Thai girls are nothing like that. I admit, they can give you one or two nights in paradise (as Stephen had put it), but as soon as you are going steady, your main squeeze turns into a tigress. Forget about loyalty, forget about submission. A cat fight for every snip of tenderness is what you get.

But Nang was different. Also she was more mature than my Pakarang pickups in the old days. It was pure luck and good fortune that I had met this wonderful lady and received her blessed love. And it wasn't that "I believe my wife" thing either. I wasn't naive and no cuckoo. I saw her like she was and I loved her for it.

So what did actually drive me to accept, or rather provoke, the challenge? At that moment I couldn't figure it out. I just knew that this was the time, the instance, the turning point. If I did not do it now, I never would.

Maybe I didn't believe in my own luck? Maybe I needed a sign from above to indemnify my decisions? Maybe I was just suffering a setback? In any case it seemed the right thing to do to leave the lures, temptations and pitfalls of Phuket paradise behind and reach for real happiness in mutuality.

Slowly I got into the water. My feet did not reach the ground. I held onto the basin's wall for a second, pondering my situation. I was alone in an alien place. I was going to swim in bottomless muddy waters into the dark cave, not knowing how deep it was, what currents there might be, what animals might frolic under the surface. As I began to float towards the opening I made a quick calculation in my mind. There were no freshwater crocodiles here. There was hardly any chance of poisonous or biting fish at this place. Insects, well. Centipedes, spiders, maybe scorpions. Snakes, certainly, but Thai snakes hardly ever interfere with man. Statistically, I assured myself, swimming into the cave was as safe as taking a nap in an airplane. It just didn't feel that way, that's all.

As soon as I passed the entry and forwarded into the shadowy part of the cave, my eyes that up till this moment had been submerged in bright sunlight could see nothing at all. It was a frightening minute, sullenly proceeding into pitch darkness and cold waters until slowly my pupils widened enough for me to faintly make out what was ahead. I felt an abysmal shiver. Thoughts were running through my head.

I had been in much worse situations before. I had looked down on kilometres of enemy rocks. I had been held at gunpoint, even heard the click of the failing weapon positioned against my forehead.

But this was different. Swimming into the unknown, dark and icy cave in Phang Nga there was no tangible threat besides my imagination. At war, problems tend to jump at you and you react instinctively or mechanically. But in this place my mind had all the time in the world to conjure monsters that originated not from the real world, but from inside my brain.

And there I had it. In this place, for the first time since my childhood, I was confronting the fears insidiously concealed in the depth of my soul.

There was a dull reflection, a drab wall sparsely lit by the distant sunlight. Beyond the wall was blackness and I heard a rising sound, like the rumble of a distant train. Current started to tuck at my legs, oddly it dragged me sidewise. Whatever was behind that greyish wall was threatening and fearful.

My reflexes anxiously bid me return, but I decided not to leave before I had accomplished some sort of success, so I opted for the wall. I was going to strike it, then turn around and swim back. Fighting the sinking feeling in my guts I approached the wall and reached out to touch it.

Later, lying in the sun while letting the warmth dry my body I reflected on what had just happened. The unforgiving agonising pull of the current close to the wall had nearly drowned me. That was not quite unexpected. Obviously there would be some risk in a hazardous dare like swimming into the unknown current of a mountain cave. But what happened immediately afterwards took me aback and shook my senses. Luckily my ancient but well trained army drill had taken over and I contented myself by the fact that I had done what I had to do and I had returned safely. I did not know what that "thing" was that had approached me and I was not going to probe either.

On my way back I enjoyed the stunning nature all around me. After the dark and minacious grotto the sunny world of the jungle was a joy to behold. Enormous buttress roots jetted wall-like up into a green roof made of leaves interspersed with blue dots of sky, while faint misty vapour from the waterfall drifted through the lush vegetation. Lianas with snake-like torsions connecting giant trees and ample ferns with flexible cords. Bamboo bushes stood erect with thick buds sprouting out of fertile soil like erotic cavernous bodies. Exotic flowers and epiphytic plants cowering in branch forks. An occasional traveller's tree like an enormous fan with every shade of green, flashing its wings like a windmill in the ever shifting patterns of sunrays.

Still there was a nagging feeling somewhere back in my spine...but I let it be drowned by sights and smells of amazing Thailand.

I had met my demons and my doubts. I was alive. I had a wonderful Thai lady to call my wife. I was blessed, I contended myself.

Arriving at the spot where I had left the girls, Nang was so beautiful as she waved her hand gracefully, displaying a sparkling smile, her body damp with moisture.

I embraced my sweetheart and hugged her, whispering into her ear "I love you".

Nang did not respond like Thai ladies going with farangs usually do - that is by pushing me away, shouting "คนโกหก" (liar). Instead she whispered back "I love you too teerak" and planted a soft kiss on my lips.

Noi laughed out loud, bashfully. It wasn't common for Thai people to show loving affection in public - in public outside the farang bars and beaches that is. But I didn't care, and Nang didn't care.

Meanwhile a happy crowd of Thai people had gathered. Sitting in the shades, imbibing som dam (papaya salad), crabs and mussels and other Thai snacks. Girls were laughing, children squeaking and the waterfall gurgled its assents. Under a row of kapok and jackfruit trees the falling waters pooled into a river. I sat and watched it flow for a while.

Time is nothing but an illusion, Einstein has said. And he was right. Suddenly time had flown by, the sun was hanging low, already the shadows from the cliff were moving toward our carpets. We had to leave.

Nang and Noi packed our belongings, we followed the path back to the parking and stuffed our things into the car. At Noi's hut Nang's mother and Lek the soldier were getting ready to prepare dinner. But at first Lek poured us a quick khao lao, indicating that in Thailand there is no sanuk without alcohol.

I accepted the drink, secretly holding my nose while imbibing the revulsive fluid. But he was wrong, of course. From the time Nang has stepped into my life I have experienced otherwise. Joy was wherever Nang was.

As I said, my alcoholic days were over. Monogamy rules!

The next day Nang and I bid our friends the jungle dwellers farewell and pulled out. Along the way we visited Wat Sua (tiger temple), a particular sacred place, where Nang wanted to "speak Buddha" as she called it.

Actually, the tiger temple was very impressive. There were no living tigers of course, just statues, but monkeys, dogs, snakes, birds and lizards.

Tucked away behind solid cliff walls, accessible only by a narrow entrance out of Jurassic Park, one never gets a hunch what to expect. A glorious series of grottos and vaults in the midst of a landscape out of prehistoric fiction movies. The forgotten land - you wouldn't be surprised to see dinosaurs and ancient raptors roaming freely. Which you do actually. Right beneath the floor of one of the monk's bamboo huts a huge monitor lizard held its siesta. The main grotto was wonderful - a giant, cool, dimly lit abyss with marble floors and slowly rotating fans on twenty meters long holders dropping down from the ceiling. A few meditating monks, some humble visitors. Nang kneeled down and exercised the local worship ceremony.

Next stop, the obligatory shoe leather and som dam at the food stall.

I knew that the following item on my personal agenda was going to strain my persuasive powers, so I made sure Nang was in a good mood before I pointed out that it would be great to enjoy the view from the fabled mountain top of the Tiger Wat.

"1237 steps!" Nang exclaimed, reading the sign "Teerak! You want to kill me?"

Thais seldom take pains like climbing a mountain or a stair - let alone 1237 steps - unless a really forceful motivation compels them to (like for instance the promise of delicious foods). But I persuaded Nang to escalate with me - in the end she gave in and armed with plastic water bottles we commenced the ascent.

We took it slow and easy, still in the cloudless and humid heat of the day it took great efforts and litres of perspiration. Soaked and feverish we arrived at the top. Immediately I was glad I had coaxed her. The view was outstanding - comparable to the view from an airplane. Flat green plains interjected by meandering streams, pried open by jutting rocks, stretching their jarred boulders against the blue skies. Even wide-winged eagles sailed majestically over the outstretched landscapes. It was magnificent. For quite some time Nang and I stood close, taking it all in. At the distant horizon I could spot the characteristically crooked rocks of Krabi. Standing on the top of Tiger Temple Mountain with my love, silently savouring the glory of this outlook, gave me a strange, but good feeling. It felt like arriving. I had arrived. Yet, I had to leave.

Just like the grotto under the waterfalls of Phang Nga had challenged me to make a stand, the horizons of Krabi beckoned me to venture further. Standing on the peak, looking out over the exotic landscape while pondering my inner life I knew I had to leave this country. Something in me had turned a page. That was the unfulfilled feeling that had nagged me back at the dark waterfall grotto.

Would Nang go with me? I looked at her and without speaking, her eyes answered "no".

Back in the shade of enormous rainforest trees around Wat Sua we sat and enjoyed a simple but sapid meal. Fried rice with green curry and a freshly opened coconut for a drink to go with it. A giant greyish shape appeared on the compounds. It was an elephant.

Nowadays elephants in Thailand and its neighbouring countries survive only for touristic reasons, so of course it was not a wild animal.

Nang gave the mahout a few Baht and made her turns under the belly of the beast while I contemplated my next move. I was not sure about Nang's imaginative "no". I wasn't even sure if I were going to pop the question. What would I do if I was compelled to choose between leaving without Nang - or staying with her?

Cutting the Cards

Arriving safely back home in Pakarang after the visit to Nang's sister's and the waterfall I prepared for my departure. I actually got as far as to winding up some ends and packing my first suitcase before I changed my mind. I had never met anybody like Nang before. And if she was determined to stay in Thailand, so be it. I wasn't going to leave her behind. And frankly I couldn't see her live in another country, either. Nang in foggy China? Nang in cold Scandinavia? Nang in furious New York? Without family, friends, palm trees, beaches, waterfalls and motorbikes?

So I cancelled my appointment and my new job in Shanghai that would have given me fortune and fame - at least that was what I had hoped for - and reset my plans. I was going to build a future with my wife in Thailand - I repeated the word "wife" in my mind to let the comprehension seep in.

But before grappling with harsh realities it was time for a vacation. Call it honeymoon.

My final trip with Nang on the pillion through the woods and jungles of the southlands up to Phang Nga Bay with its rugged limestone cliffs was wonderful. We had a great time, acting like children, running on emerald beaches, chasing coral fish in the bays, looking for baby morays under the abandoned coral stocks at low tide, catching fish and crabs in the poodles with bare hands... We even rode a long tail boat to the tourist traps. James Bond Island, Muslim Village, Treasure Cove ...

I felt at ease. Like arriving at fourth base. The waterfall challenge and the Krabi decision calmed down to a distant dream while utter joy of life filled my senses. I watched Nang in her sarong, buying tidbits at the food stalls, Nang in her bikini, frolicking in the waves, Nang in her evening robe, gracefully accepting a glass of champagne in a night club while a jazz band played Stella by Starlight in the background. Nang naked in the nights, swivelling a half turn before letting herself fall into the bed and embracing me with her soft arms.

But nothing lasts forever. Leisure time always flies, vacations are always too short, and honeymoons, I discovered, were a memory even before they had begun.

Back in Pakarang we tentatively began a daily routine of some sort. But mostly, we made plans for the future.

"Let's open a restaurant" Nang said.

"Why not" I replied, although the life of a restaurant patron did not seem alluring.

"I will have my sister and her family come and live with us" Nang mused "Noi can work in the kitchen for us..."

As yet I didn't have to take Nang's plans all too seriously. I was happy that she was happy planning away but who knew what ideas she would have the next day...

So I let my mind rest and decided to let things work themselves out. Whatever was going to happen it was alright with me, as long as I had Nang by my side.

So what if she would open a restaurant, in any case my able life companion would handle the matter herself and my sole contribution was going to be pecuniary - if at all.

So far I had no firm plans besides staying with Nang unconditionally, no matter what, no matter how. I didn't know what we were going to do, but in my heart I felt convinced that the future would find her own sweet way. I would just have to let it roll. I resumed writing. At home. With my wife.

"What had happened to the old Fox?" you may ask, the one on the prowl, always out there, flying beautiful girls to the moon and worshipping curvaceous Go Go dancers?

Well, I am sure he was still around somewhere, but I guess he was on vacation, maybe even retired. Especially after I got the message that Nang was pregnant. I was going to be the father of a child... that was wild.

I went out and bought a ring for Nang - of the ostentatious kind Thai girls like so much. I had planned to give it to her the following week, at our first anniversary.

But life does not always play by the rules. A couple of days later the US Navy was paying a visit to the island again and a battleship entered Pakarang Bay. As always the girls were wild with anticipation of glorious days ahead with handsome, tall, long-nosed, blonde soldiers coming to town with erect weapons aiming straight at the core of Thai womanhood.

The whole town vibrated with an expectant tenseness as the profile of the warship grew bigger and finally dropped anchor a few hundred metres from the beach.

"Teerak, I go to the Love Me Bar and talk to my friends" Nang said casually, as we were finishing supper.

"What is happening?" I asked, surprised.

Nang hadn't been to any bar since we had returned from our travel. I knew she still had a few friends down in Bangla, but I had actually expected that with our new life in togetherness those days were gone.

"Are you going to meet a handsome US navy boy?" I asked with a grin that was intended to be mischievous.

"Teerak, don't speak like that" Nang said and looked at me unsmilingly.

"You know you can trust me. You are only one for me."

But that night, Nang did not come home. In the morning I awoke alone. I was surprised, but I didn't worry. Until I heard somebody's hard knocking and the door being flung open.

Gaew rushed in, her face distorted by horror. She was barely able to control her voice and she trembled as she sputtered the words she was trying to say, so loud it hurt my ears.

"Nang!" she bawled "Nang dead! Nang die!"

Her body shook with convulsions. I took her hands and slowly and deliberately I asked her to please calm down.

"Shh... easy now. What is happening? What is the problem? Is Nang OK?"

"No, she not OK. She dead already!"

At that moment I was still convinced that Nang was alright. Sure, something might have happened, maybe a motorbike accident, she might even be in hospital...

But by Gaew's desperate looks and stammering words finally the horrid truth sunk in.

What happened next is all in a flurry. Probably Gaew and I rode a bike to the hospital's mortuary and probably somebody - me? - identified the corpse.

Nang.

Nang, my love... though unspoken she had indicated she wouldn't go with me if I decided to leave Thailand, I had not expected her to die on me, now that I had decided to join fate with her and stay put. I had voted against my Krabi compulsion and decided to stay - as I just couldn't imagine living without Nang any more. But cruelly now fate had made the unimaginable come true.

I hang out with her friends for a few days while the investigators examined the case, staying drunk all the time. Before going on with my life, before doing any-thing, I wanted to know what had happened. Rumours and details started to make the rounds. Nang had been shot. With a handgun. By a US navy officer. At the Love Me Bar.

At least she had not been shot while with a man in a hotel bed or any other bed. I clung to her statement that I had been her "only one". Not that it mattered much. I would have forgiven her, even if she...

I blamed myself for her death. Probably if I had followed the signs and done what my intuition had intended, if I had left, Nang would not be dead by now.

I tried to continuously drown my pain with Jack Daniel's but it didn't work. Life had lost its flavour and sleeping alone - if at all - was pure hell... so for some time I even let Ning and Gaew comfort me in a way that Thai girls can do so well...

Back in the old days being the male part of that trio would have made my endocrine elevation go wild but in the present situation I hardly noticed the girls being around.

Having met death and meaningless violence in my for-mer life in the army and even on the streets and in the bars of present Thailand I was not the one to phrase the equally mindless question "God, why?" or "God, why me?" But still I urgently felt the need to see Nang's killer and look him in the eye. Don't ask me why. I just did.

So I acted.

Through some connections and by means of a lump sum of money I got access to jail and the man that had shot my love. I don't know why he had agreed to meet me. I don't know what they had told him. Or threatened him with.

I didn't feel hate. Not even resent. I just felt the need to meet the guy and get it over with, so I could go on with my life, somehow. I even shook hands with him. His insignia showed the rank of a commanding officer.

My first question was: "Why did you shoot her?"

He said: "I love her."

Strangely, that changed it. Now I did feel hate mounting inside my guts.

"Is that why you shot her? Because you loved her?"

"Honestly, I wasn't myself, when that happened. I know I am guilty and I face life in prison or a death sentence... But looking back at the scene I see somebody else taking out the gun and shooting it... into her face..."

We both looked out of the window in silence without seeing.

"I loved her, but she did not love me back. I have divorced my wife for her. I had arranged for the money, we could have lived where ever she would choose..."

He retracted his glance and looked at me.

"But there was another guy. She said she loved him more. She had changed her plans."

"The other guy is me" I said.

"Yes, I thought so."

The Navy officer clenched his fists and gritted his teeth for a moment.

"You know, you and me are not the only ones. Not by far. It was easy to fall in love with her..."

His face tightened and his eyes obtained a strange hardness.

"I should have shot you instead" he said in a flat voice and shook his head.

There was a guard by the door, but the man was inattentive, almost asleep. I wrenched the machine gun out of his hands and succeeded to hit the Navy officer in the head with the shaft several times before they stopped me.

Wisely they didn't put me in a cell with the Navy commander, but I had to share the night with about a dozen other inmates, mostly Thais and a pair of young French guys, who were involved in a fatal motorbike accident.

It was not so bad. I could buy my way out the next day and in the meantime I was so numbed by Nang's death that I didn't care much where or who I was. In the end I paid the inattentive guard a small fortune to take the rap. That way everybody came out of it fairly well - and that was it so far.

Back at my house the girls still managed to combine the sorrow of life with the joy of living - as Thai people can do and I could not. They also enjoyed the sex as always. Somehow to them it all made sense, I guess. Or maybe they just did not have that burdensome access to that idiotic search for meaningfulness and cosmic orderliness that plagued my Western mind.

I felt neither joy in sex nor relief in the fact that I had met the murderer and hit him in the head. I remember sitting in Laan Sukapok early one morning with Gaew, watching the golden girls drift up from the bars. It was the usual glorious scenery... but in my mind nothing was the same and everything seemed plainly dull and grey.

The pain went on. So I figured I might as well make an effort to make it stop. Either that or die.

I decided to cut the cards. I took my bike, the Harley this time, not the Suzi. It seemed proper to let another American decide the matter - and drove along the winding beach road all the way to its end up to the top of the mountain at Cap Laem Yanoi. I left the bike in the parking lot, climbed the steep slope and sat on top of the cliff watching the sun go down over the Andaman Sea and the unnamed little uninhabited island just a mile off the shore before it disappeared in this little green flash.

Several busloads of tourists had watched the spectacle from the balustrades beneath the spot where I was. They were busy leaving the place and as the last of the buses had left I sat quietly a few moments until it was pitch dark. I then scrambled back to the parking, opened my bottle of Jack Daniels' and emptied it with one long gulp.

I don't remember what happened during the rest of that night. For me it had been a straight gamble, tossing coins, live or die. Whatever the outcome - and I had figured it to be less than fifty, a lot less - I desperately needed to terminate the evil limbo I was in.

Riding the hazardous slope down Laem Mountain and the sinuous road back to Pakarang on a heavy bike was a dangerous challenge even in bright daylight.

But in the dark - there were no lamp posts in this part of the country - in the occasional rain on slippery asphalt - rainy season was setting in - and stoned out of my mind it was less than an even bet whether I would survive or not. I had set my mind at riding fast and taking risks. Either I would wake up unhurt the next day or preferably I would be dead. What I did not want, was to wake up in a wheel chair...

As I said, I don't remember what happened that night. But I awoke at home with Gaew and Porn in my bed the very next day. I didn't even have a hangover. Obviously I was alive and remarkably well, not in a wheel chair that is. I had a bruised knee, I felt a certain stiffness in my loins and an itching in my nose, that was all. I wondered where the bike was and how it looked. I got out of the bed and went out to the front porch. The Harley stood parked on its sidestand. It was wet even though standing in the sun, obviously there had been a passing shower - I could see a dark anvil cloud in the distance. Rainy season was on its way.

So I had gambled the dice and destiny had decided that I shalt live.

In the bathroom the mirror informed me that my nose was broken. That explained the itch. Well - I was going to deal with that later.

In the bedroom the two girls were sound asleep. I noticed a pool of blood on the sheets. From my broken nose? But no, in the mirror there had been no blood in my face at all. My face had been swept clean. Actually I discovered that there was a wad of cotton in my nostrils - somebody must have looked after me before putting me to bed.

Examining the bed and the girls I found that the stains were not from my nose but from Gaew. Her period, that was all. I left the sleeping girls - judging by their deep hypnosis and methylated smell they too had had more than a few drinks last night - and sat down in the rocking chair on the patio.

Sugar canes, banana plants and passion flowers in the garden, a barking dog, the characteristic watery bubble sound from an old Honda Dream exhaust pipe down under, steamy mist raising from the tree tops on the mountains...

Should I venture to the Laan Sukapok and start my day with a drink? I decided against it. Life as I had known it had lost not only its thrill but also its momentum.

"At least momentarily" I reassured myself. The fact that Nang's life had ended did not end my life too, even if it felt that way. I had cut the cards, I had survived the quest. Life was going on and that meant I would have to take a new stand. In the back of my mind I knew I was going to fight my way back to the living. Sensation, emotion... one day I would have it all back, might even find a new love...But not here.

So I left paradise.

Everybody knows that even in paradise there has to be a snake and a harbinger of Evil. Living in paradise is never for ever. At some point fall of man and expulsion will take place...

I didn't keep the ring. I gave it to Noi, Nang's sister. I knew she was going to pawn it eventually, but I didn't care. All I kept was just one picture of Nang and me in my wallet.

I didn't even stay for her funeral. I just couldn't. Seeing her remains end up in smoke and vanish in the air was not bearable. It would have confirmed her death and the end of things.

4. FOX FAQ

Before answering your questions I would like to relay Harry's own comment on his book:

"My name is Harry "Fox" James and before you ask, what with the middle name, here is the story: I am a vet and during the war against terrorism they used to call me the Fox because I was a reliable brother in arms, especially at night patrols. Also I took great pains watching my tail, you see. That is why I survived, even without much injury. Except from a little shell wound that still aches once in a while.

But that is not the interesting part. At least not for my readers I guess. Having a journalistic background I did some blogging while living on the rock in Andaman Thailand. And everybody kept telling me to hard copy the stuff. So finally, now I did with the helping hand of a friend. If you enjoy reading it just half as much as I did writing when going through the motions, I know you will have a heck of a time. Except for the ending, that is... But of course I don't have to tell you that even paradise does not contain eternal happiness.

The stories are mostly located shortly before the big T hit in 2004, so we are in the good old settings when sex and fun were abundant, before all those new buildings and malls rose to stardom and ugly fame. And before the horrid stench...

I left after the Tsunami that killed some of my best friends (and bars). Oddly that felt more of a loss than even losing the partners that were wasted during the war.

And... to be honest, the loss of Nang was the worst of all. I migrated further to the East and another odd thing, in Vietnam I feel more at home than in Thailand, even than in the Americas. Maybe it is all the leavings that still remain after the French and American wars here. All those bad old shells, still waiting to go off. Once a vet, always a vet I guess."

Some of you have emailed Harry and asked questions about him as a person. I have been talking to him about it, but he said...

"I believe my private life does not concern the public, even though the stories are about me and my experiences in Thailand. I was just writing those stories for the fun of it. And to make a living, of course. I welcome every reader who enjoys them. I even welcome the readers, who hate 'em. You know what I mean - love or hate, as long as there is some emotion or sense of thrill. I am happy to share some of my insights, but as far as my own self is concerned - I don't feel my age, my size or the amount of money in my wallet has much to do with what I write."

For those of you, who are disappointed by Harry's seclusiveness - let me satisfy your curiosity a little bit. Knowing Harry Fox quite well, I have taken the liberty to answer a few questions and clarifying a few points. So - here are some answers to some of the most frequently asked Harry Fox questions.

Has Harry Fox written other books?

Yes. Even though Harry is a journalist and not a novelist I know that Harry has written e.g. "The Girl from Punta Arenas". But the issues have long been sold out. Harry claims he doesn't even own a copy himself.

"I lent my last copy to a friend and I never got it back" he told me.

Mike says that Harry has written several other books. Some of them with peculiar subjects like "Out of In" and "The Sex of Zen". I will ask Harry next time I see him. By the way, "Another Night in Paradise" is the first book that Harry wrote under a pen name (mine).

Has Harry Fox ever doubled James Bond?

I have heard those rumours, but people the likes of Harry Fox enjoy to be shrouded in mystery. I wouldn't believe those exaggerations. As far as I know, Harry's encounters with Pierce Brosnan and Roger Moore were limited to a certain bar in Phuket Town. I since met several ladies who claim that they have spent wild nights with the three gentlemen, but as everybody knows, Pierce and Roger were absolutely true and faithful to their wives.

In my opinion, there might be more truth in the anecdotes about Harry and Claude Van Damme, though. At the time Van Damme was shooting on Phuket, he was heavily into sex and drugs, so I guess a lot of partying was going down...

On a similar matter - concerning the rumours about "The Beach" (with Leonardo de Caprio) - I asked Harry if he was the real author of the script and he flatly said "no". But gruntily he admitted that he had been asked to add some locally flavoured parts to the original script. The double doing Leonardo's swimming, though, is - would you believe it - our own Mike Björklund, manager of Fode Language Phuket. Not that he was a real stuntman, but obviously his vital body parts matched that of Leo's.

Is Harry Fox into motorbikes?

Sure. Like everybody else on the island, Harry went about on a bike. He rode a Honda Dream on a daily basis and bought a chopper for trips outside Pakarang. Mike says Harry owns a beautiful black Harley Davidson "Fat Boy", but I have only seen him on his red Suzuki Intruder - "cause they're plainly more reliable" as he said.

Is Harry Fox his real name?

Yes - and "Another Night in Paradise" is the first of his books written under a pen name.

Is Harry Fox into ladies?

Are you joking? You only have to read one single of his stories to realize that there is nothing Harry adores more than the female sex.

Is Harry Fox an alcoholic?

I understand why one would ask this question. Alcohol, and preferably Jack Daniel's whisky seem to play a big role in Harry's blog. But it was just a phase, I think. In the night life paradise of Pakarang alcoholic drinks abound everywhere. And of course after Nang died Harry was going through a period of heavy drinking. Understandably, I think, others might have taken medical support, or their own life... But as far as I know, that was it. When I met him at a writers' convention in Shanghai a couple of years after Nang's death he was absolutely sober.

Is Harry Fox a katheoy?

No, he is a woman. Sorry, just kidding! Harry, of course, is pure chauvinist male through and through.

Is Harry Fox an American?

Yes, he is a registered citizen of Brazil (gotcha!). At least according to the passport I saw once. But it may be a fake and I guess at least at a certain time he must have been a citizen of the USA, since he gronked the shit out of North African terrorists as a US soldier.

Does Harry Fox really live on Phuket?

Not any more. And forget the anecdotes about Harry living in a Go Go bar. At the time of writing he resided in a house on Nanai. Mike says that Harry owns at least two other domiciles somewhere around the world. I wouldn't be surprised.

Is Harry Fox married?

Yes. To his laptop, a slim little IBM and they have maintained a fulfilling relationship for several decades.

What kind of education does Harry have?

As far as I know Harry worked as an investigative journalist before and after his army stint. Other than that - I talked to a friend of Harry's, a medical doctor, who knows Harry from way back. He told me that Harry had actually worked in a medical corps. He couldn't say whether Harry has taken any medical exams, though.
"To be honest, I doubt it" he said. "But Harry was a good paramedic."

Has Harry ever given any interviews?

No - with one exception. CNN was on the island to report on some touristic stuff and they caught wind of Harry being there so they decided to interview him on a side line. But the interview was never aired, it was too short, because Harry broke it off. He told me later that the interviewer had lectured him heavily about moral and prostitution issues without really listening to what Harry had to say. So Harry rose from his chair and left, wordlessly. I have that little snip on my hard drive, though and here it is:

CNN: Harry Fox, you are known to be very reluctant to go public. What changed your mind this time?

HF: Well, first of all it depends on who is doing the publicizing. I have been giving the possibility to view the material and to make changes, if I feel it's appropriate.

CNN: You have chosen to live in South East Asia most of the year. Doesn't it bother you that Thailand has a reputation of being a sex-tourist destination?

HF: Sure does. Because people have it the wrong way round. Tourism is not fortifying the dirty prostitutional oppression of innocent young girls. Tourism is actually heightening the living standards and the quality of the poor. Actually if somebody is being exploited here, it is the tourists, not the girls.

CNN: How is that?

HF: You wouldn't believe how much of the income from tourism and what Western media call "sex-business" is going straight to the most underdeveloped parts of Thailand and neighbouring countries. I have never seen foreign money influx in any so-called third world or underdeveloped or even poor country being distributed so socially fair and equitable. That money is going straight into the poor folks pockets.

CNN: Do you really mean that? Last night one of our reporters was in the Go Go bars and he saw little girls the age of fifteen brutally be taken advantage of by exploitative mongers and mamasans.

HF: Isn't that remarkable... I have been living here for more than a decade, I have been to every A Go Go in this place dozens of times, I know most of their owners... and neither I nor any of my friends have ever noticed fifteen year old girls in those places. I find it odd that you reporters come here and on the first day you reveal adiabatic conditions that neither natives nor old hands and expats have ever seen nor heard of?

HF: Listen, Mr Fox, I can't believe that you sit there and deny facts...

At this point the conversation broke up as Harry picked up his sunglasses and left.

ANOTHER NIGHT IN PARADISE